JUVENAL
Satires I, III, X

Edited with Introduction and Notes by
Niall Rudd
(Emeritus Professor of Latin, University of Bristol)
and
Edward Courtney
(Gildersleeve Professor of Latin, University of Virginia)

Bristol Classical Press

This impression 2002
Second edition 1982
First published in 1977 by
Bristol Classical Press
an imprint of
Gerald Duckworth & Co. Ltd.
61 Frith Street, London W1D 3JL
Tel: 020 7434 4242
Fax: 020 7434 4420
inquiries@duckworth-publishers.co.uk
www.ducknet.co.uk

© 1977, 1982 by N. Rudd and E. Courtney

A catalogue record for this book is available
from the British Library

ISBN 0 906515 03 3

Printed and bound in Great Britain by
Antony Rowe Ltd, Eastbourne

Cover illustration: the Emperor Domitian

CONTENTS

PREFACE TO THE SECOND EDITION

This was the first volume published by the Bristol Classical Press and, as such, was something of an experiment. Our intention was to provide a 'utility' edition with condensed and economical notes at a realistic price. As there have been four reprints in the last five years the book seems to have served its purpose reasonably well. But it has been suggested that, since Juvenal is so difficult a poet, more help should be given to the reader. And so some ninety notes have now been added and a few earlier notes modified. We have not included critical essays on the poems (for that would have increased the price considerably), but we have slightly expanded the introduction and added a few items to the bibliography — including the large commentary by E.C. mentioned in the Preface to the First Edition. Typescript and layout have been totally revised.

April 1982 N.R.
E.C.

PREFACE TO FIRST EDITION

The purpose of this elementary commentary is to help sixth formers and undergraduates to understand Juvenal's meaning. A good deal of attention has been paid to grammar, and where it seemed useful reference has been made to Gildersleeve and Lodge, *Latin Grammar*, reissued 1971 (GL) and to E. C. Woodcock, *A New Latin Syntax*, 1959 (W). Historical points are explained as briefly as possible, and apart from a few general remarks in the introduction there is little in the way of literary appreciation. These wider areas of scholarship can be explored with the aid of the bibliography.

The text differs from the Oxford Classical Text in about forty places, but many of the changes are in minor details of spelling or punctuation. The notes are, of course, largely tralaticious; but a comparison with the editions of Mayor, Friedlaender, and Duff will show that there has been a good deal of selection and compression. Most of what is new is derived from an extensive commentary by E.C. which is nearing completion. We have both worked through the present selection and take joint responsibility for the views expressed. The main points on which we differ have been indicated in the notes.

May 1977 N.R.
E.C.

INTRODUCTION

Decimus[1] Iunius Iuvenalis came from Aquinum, a town some eighty miles south east of Rome (3.319–320). The date of his birth is unknown and we have to make do with some very crude estimates. In an epigram of Martial's published in A.D. 92 (7.91) he is called *facundus* – a word which probably means 'eloquent' here rather than 'poetic'. A reputation for eloquence might have been achieved at an early age, so could Juvenal have been born about A.D. 70? Hardly, for in a passage written about 124 (*Sat.* 11.201–203) he contrasts himself with the young, speaking of his 'wrinkled skin'; such an expression would sound slightly odd coming from a man of fifty-four. It may be argued that Juvenal frequently exaggerates, but there is also another point which tells against so late a date. In *Epig.* 7.24 Martial, who was born about A.D.41, compares his friendship with Juvenal to the friendships of Orestes and Pylades, Agamemnon and Menelaus, and Castor and Pollux. Even allowing for literary convention this hardly suggests that he was speaking of a man thirty years his junior. Suppose, then, we choose a much earlier year – say A.D.50. That too cannot be disproved, but if we accept a date of 110 or a little later for the appearance of Book 1 it is *a priori* unlikely that Juvenal was over sixty when he began to publish his satires. And so we may settle without much confidence on an intermediate date of about A.D.60.

The facts known about Juvenal's life are equally scanty. He tells us himself that he received a secondary education (1.15–17). Later, about A.D.101, he is visualized by his friend Martial, who had by now returned to Spain, as wandering restlessly along the Subura and trudging up hill to the houses of rich patrons (12.18). This shows that the pictures of the client's life given in the satires were drawn, however indirectly, from personal experience. It is usually stated that at some time in his career Juvenal visited Egypt, but this is based on what may be a misinterpret-

---

1. The evidence for the poet's praenomen is less solid than is often assumed.

ation of *Sat.* 15.45.[1] What we can say is that in the later part of his life he had a modest house in Rome, which he had apparently inherited (12.87–89), and a small farm at Tibur (11.65 and 69).

Two other questions are usually discussed in connection with Juvenal's life: (a) whether the Iuvenalis who made a dedication to Ceres[2] at Aquinum is to be identified with the poet, and (b) whether the account of his exile is trustworthy. The dedicator of the inscription was a well-to-do local magistrate and a *flamen* of the deified Vespasian. He had also apparently been tribune of a miliary cohort (i.e. a cohort of a thousand men) raised in Dalmatia. It is not very easy to square these details with our picture of the satirist. Moreover, it seems that miliary cohorts of Dalmatians were first formed in the Marcomannic wars of Marcus Aurelius (A.D.167–180).[3] If this is true, the inscription must have been dedicated by a younger kinsman.

The tradition that Juvenal was exiled by the emperor for attacking a court favourite is found in several scholia dating from the fourth century, in Sidonius Apollinaris who was writing in the fifth century, and in a Life which may well be later still. The story has a number of variations, but its kernel has been accepted by Highet and Green (see bibliography) and the reader will find an interesting reconstruction of Juvenal's career in their works. In the present editors' view, however, the tradition raises so many difficulties that it cannot be used as evidence.

Of the satires in Book 1 (i.e. nos. 1–5) 3 and 5 are undatable; *Sat.* 2.102–103 probably refers to Tacitus' *Histories* all of which had appeared by about A.D.109, and so the poem belongs to that time or shortly after; *Sat.* 1.49-50 mentions the prosecution of Marius Priscus

1. The passage runs as follows:

horrida sane
Aegyptos, sed luxuria, quantum ipse notavi,
barbara famoso non cedit turba Canopo.

Egypt is certainly rough, but when it comes to self-indulgence ... the barbarous rabble is just as bad as the notorious citizens of Canopus.

When *quantum ipse notavi* is taken as the equivalent of *ut ipse notavi* ('as I myself have observed') this produces an emphatic statement which would support the hypothesis that Juvenal had been in Egypt. But there is no satisfactory evidence for the equation of *quantum* and *ut* in Juvenal's time, and it is better to translate 'as far as I myself have observed'. This does not corroborate but rather qualifies the main statement (*non cedit*). And it could be based simply on Juvenal's observation of Egyptians in Rome.

2. Reports of the inscription agree on the letters *RI*. One scholar thought he could also see the initial *C*; but we cannot be sure that he was right, and his restoration *CereRI* could have been based on his recollection of *Sat.* 3.320 which mentions a cult of Ceres at Aquinum (but connects it with a name other than Juvenal's). The inscription no longer survives.

3. See J. J. Wilkes, *Dalmatia* (1969) 141 and 473.

(A.D.100), but the reference may have been prompted by Pliny's account of the trial in *Epist.* 2.11 which was not published until about 104. This still does not enable us to place the satire, for the memory of that notorious case would have lasted for several years. Moreover, the programmatic character of *Sat.* 1 tends to indicate that most of the other pieces in the book had already been written. When these points are taken in conjunction with the date of Book 2 (A.D.116–117) we are left with a date of about 110–112 for the publication of Book 1.

Our third poem, *Sat.* 10, which with 11 and 12 makes up Book 4, cannot be dated internally. However, as the latest reference in Book 3 is to about 120 (assuming that Hadrian is the emperor mentioned in 7.1), and as the earliest firm reference in Book 5 is to 127 (assuming that Fonteius in 13.17 is the consul of 67), it is reasonable to put *Sat.* 10 somewhere about 123.[1] As for the last satires, the reference to the consul Iuncus in 15.27 means that the poem is later than A.D.127. Of *Sat.* 16 only sixty lines have survived. Either it was unfinished at Juvenal's death or else the remainder was lost at an early stage of the tradition. It looks, then, as if the poet stopped writing about A.D.130.

To sum up. Juvenal was born in the reign of Nero (A.D.54–68), spent his teens under Vespasian (A.D.69–79) and his early manhood under Domitian (A.D.81-96). He began to write in the reign of Trajan (A.D.98–117) and finished under Hadrian (A.D.117–138). The date of his death is uncertain. In reading the satires it is naturally desirable to have some knowledge of their historical background. The worst periods in the reigns of Tiberius, Nero, and Domitian are especially important since Juvenal draws most of his examples from them.

The main problem in understanding Juvenal, however, is not historical but literary. What was he trying to accomplish in his satires, and how are we supposed to take them? There are no simple answers to these questions, but the following guidelines may be helpful:

1.   Did Juvenal intend to promote general moral reform?

Most of those who have written about Juvenal over the centuries think he did. Ramsay (Loeb translation xxxiii–xxxiv) says: 'He holds up a mirror to every part of the private life of the Rome of his day, and by the most caustic and trenchant invective seeks to shame her out of her vices'. Gifford (Introduction to his translation of 1802) assures us that 'he laboured . . . to set forth the loveliness of virtue and the deformity and horror of vice in full and perfect display'. Lubinus in 1603 declared that

---

1. There is a reference in *Sat.* 14.196 to campaigns against the Moors and the Brigantes, which indicates that the satire must have been written within a few years of A.D.120. But this is not precise enough to help us.

Juvenal contained a greater amount of sound moral teaching than the whole of Aristotle's *Nicomachean Ethics*. Britannicus in 1501 claimed that Juvenal's stern morality made his satires an ideal school text. From there we go back to the middle ages, when Juvenal stood so high as a preacher and moralist that he was sometimes referred to simply as *ethicus*.

Yet such positive intentions are seldom evident. It is true that in the first part of *Sat.* 8 Juvenal urges a governor designate to match his noble birth with his conduct; in *Sat.* 11 Juvenal's old-fashioned hospitality shows how to avoid extravagance; *Sat.* 13 dilates on the terrors of a guilty conscience; and *Sat.* 14 condemns parents who do not set a good example. But these passages are not typical. The limited importance of didacticism can be seen if we ask whether the portrait of Virro (*Sat.* 5) was intended to bring about a general improvement in the manners of hosts, whether many women were likely to become more virtuous on reading *Sat.* 6, and whether new, enlightened, patrons were expected to emerge as a result of *Sat.* 7. Most of the features of Roman life attacked by Juvenal were the result of a long and irreversible process. The squalor and danger of *insulae*, the impoverishment of the middle class, the success of energetic freedmen and immigrants, the sexual frivolity — these were developments which could not possibly have been altered by the work of a poet. And Juvenal knew it:

> *nil erit ulterius quod nostris moribus addat*
> *posteritas, eadem facient cupientque minores.*

> (*Sat.* 1.147–148)

2.   Was it, then, Juvenal's primary intention to express his indignation and disgust at the vicious society in which he lived? Here we must draw a distinction. From his study of the names in the satires Sir Ronald Syme concludes that 'Juvenal does not attack any person or category that commands influence in his own time'.[1] Instead he does something different: he uses notorious characters from earlier generations as *exempla* to illustrate crimes and vices which are, for the most part, still flourishing. As he says at the end of his programmatic satire:

> *experiar quid concedatur in illos*
> *quorum Flaminia tegitur cinis atque Latina.*

> (*Sat.* 1.170–171)

This procedure doubtless gave Juvenal some degree of protection; but we

1. R. Syme, *Tacitus* (1958) vol. 2, 778.

ought not to make the further assumption that because the satires contained no important (living) names they were incapable of causing offence. Under Trajan and Hadrian, for example, several men of Greek extraction held influential positions. What would they have thought of *Sat*. 3? And how many Roman ladies gave their unqualified approval to *Sat*. 6?

3.   If he didn't hope to remedy these evils, should Juvenal then be thought of more as a declaimer, giving a display of rhetorical virtuosity?

There is a good deal of truth in this. We know from *Sat*. 1 that Juvenal had received a rhetorical education, and his poems exhibit all the attendant features from anaphora to zeugma (GL 688–700). The school handbooks provided a range of general topics such as the *locus de divitiis*, the *locus de fortuna*, and the *locus de saeculo* (on the degeneracy of the age), and also a wealth of illustration drawn from the lives of the notorious or the unfortunate. Thanks to the appearance of the Loeb translation of the elder Seneca we now have easier access to the world of declamations, and we need not look much further to find the source of Juvenal's general ideas. In spite of a few references to Stoicism and Epicureanism, he did not possess a philosophical mind (see 13.120 ff); and so unlike Horace, he does not ask us to discriminate between one type of fault and another. Everything is condemned with the same vehemence. This too is part of his rhetorical stance. Again, as he is not conversing with us in an easy informal way, he does not tell us about his friends or his private life; instead he stands apart and delivers a series of harangues. The most famous of these (with the exception of *Sat*. 10) are inspired by *indignatio* – a term which in the vocabulary of rhetoric can imply not just indignation on the part of the speaker but also a rhetorical procedure for arousing the same emotion in the reader (see Cicero, *De inventione* 1.100–105).

Yet it would be wrong to think of Juvenal simply as a declaimer. Leaving aside the *poetic* quality of his writings (which lifts them into quite a different dimension) we cannot always fit the satires into any of the conventional rhetorical categories.[1] Clearly they are not examples of the *genus iudiciale* (the satirist is not arguing a case in court or appealing to any particular law); nor can they be related very closely to the *genus deliberativum*, or its school version the *suasoria*. True, *Sat*. 3 marshalls reasons for leaving Rome and *Sat*. 6 for eschewing marriage, but several others (e.g. 2, 4, and 7) are not constructed in that way, and even *Sat*. 1

1. See W. S. Anderson, *Yale Classical Studies* 17 (1961) 37–51, and E. J. Kenney, *Latomus* 22 (1963), 704–720.

does not try to persuade anyone else to write satire. In some respects — especially in their abundant *vituperatio* — the satires come closest to the *genus demonstrativum* (which was largely concerned with praise or blame); but the standard examples of vituperative oratory, like Caesar's *Anticato* or Cicero's *In Pisonem*, were composed for particular occasions and directed at specific people. It is hard to think of any speech or group of speeches that would correspond to the first two books of Juvenal in structure and function.

Or in wit. For in his own dreadful way Juvenal is an immensely entertaining writer, which is more than can be said for any of the surviving declaimers. His best pieces communicate a sense of energy and exhilaration which is at odds with their pessimistic message. And one comes to feel that in a rather perverse way Juvenal *needs* Rome. In *Sat.* 3, after all, it is Umbricius who leaves, not the poet. Again, Juvenal's wit is often so extravagant, and sometimes so inappropriate to his thesis, that we can hardly believe his indignation to be quite sincere.[1] But sincerity — or the appearance of sincerity — is an orator's main business. If he is willing to weaken his argument for the sake of a joke, his effectiveness is seriously diminished. This consideration also prevents us from assessing Juvenal's satire wholly in terms of anger and disgust.

4.   Should we, then, regard Juvenal primarily as a wit?

This is the position worked out with skill and learning by H. A. Mason, who sets out to show that Juvenal is 'more interested in literature than in social conditions, and that he lacks any consistent stand-point or moral coherence. Indeed his whole art consists in opportunism and the surprise effects obtainable from deliberate inconsistency'.[2] In taking this approach Mason starts from Martial, arguing that both he and Juvenal shared an audience which, while not necessarily vicious, enjoyed salacious poetry as a kind of game, provided it was cleverly written. He then shows how Juvenal sometimes used stones from Martial's epigrams to construct the more elaborate edifice of his own satires. Thus *Epig.* 3.30 lies behind *Sat.* 1.117ff. and *Epig.* 4.5 supplies the idea for *Sat.* 3.41ff.

All this is true and worth saying. Yet it would be wrong to under-estimate the firm foundation of fact which often underlies even the most hyperbolic passages. The tedium and hypocrisy of recitations, the fires and falling houses, discrimination in hospitality, the plight of intellectuals,

---

1. See e.g. *Sat.* 3.12, 92–3 and 127–36.

2. H. A. Mason, *Critical Essays on Roman Literature*, ed. J. P. Sullivan (1963) 107.

the unpopularity of the army — these and many other features of Roman life are abundantly attested in other sources.[1]

Nor, after all, can we neglect the moral element in the satires. Here it may look as if we have come full circle; but to express and appeal to an attitude of mind is only indirectly connected with influencing behaviour; and to invite a moral response from the reader is very different from trying to reform society. At the end of *Sat.* 4, after describing the farcical council-meeting about Domitian's fish, Juvenal suddenly says:

> *atque utinam his potius nugis tota illa dedisset*
> *tempora saevitiae, claras quibus abstulit urbi*
> *inlustresque animas inpune et vindice nullo.*

> (*Sat.* 4.150—152)

No irony there. Or again, near the end of *Sat.* 2, which deals with effeminate hypocrites *qui Curios simulant et Bacchanalia vivunt*, Juvenal turns to the reader and asks:

> *Curius quid sentit et ambo*
> *Scipiadae, quid Fabricius manesque Camilli,*
> *quid Cremerae legio et Cannis consumpta iuventus,*
> *tot bellorum animae, quotiens hinc talis ad illos*
> *umbra venit? cuperent lustrari, si qua darentur*
> *sulpura cum taedis et si foret umida laurus.*

> (*Sat.* 2.153—158)

The same contempt is implicit in *Sat.* 9. Nor was Juvenal incapable of indignation at the end of his career. If *Sat.* 16 is not a genuine protest against the army then why was it written? Certainly the sophisticated audience which enjoyed Martial would have had little sympathy with those hobnailed centurions.

These remarks may help to define the area within which a critical assessment of Juvenal has to be made. How the final judgement is composed and weighted must be left to the reader after he has followed the path of this complex and elusive genius.

---

1. Mayor's notes are an invaluable collection of comparative material.

BIBLIOGRAPHY
(other titles are mentioned in the notes)

Adams, J.N., *The Latin Sexual Vocabulary*, Duckworth 1982.

Anderson, W.S., *Essays on Roman Satire*, Princeton 1982.

Balsdon, J.P.V.D., *Life and Leisure in Ancient Rome*, Bodley Head 1969.

——— *Romans and Aliens*, Duckworth 1979.

Bonner, S.F., *Education in Ancient Rome*, Methuen 1977.*

Bramble, J., 'Martial and Juvenal', *The Cambridge History of Classical Literature*, vol. 2, Cambridge 1982, 597-623

Braund, S., *Beyond Anger*, Cambridge 1988.*

——— S.M., *Juvenal. Satires, Book I*, Cambridge 1996

Clausen, W.V., *A. Persi Flacci et D. Iuni Iuuenalis Saturae*, revised edn, Oxford 1992.

Coffey, M., *Roman Satire*, 2nd edn, Bristol Classical Press 1989.

Courtney, E., *A Commentary on the Satires of Juvenal*, Athlone Press 1980.

——— 'The progress of emendation in the text of Juvenal since the Renaissance', *Aufstieg und Niedergang der römischen Welt* 33.1, 1989, 824-47.

Ferguson, J. *Juvenal: the Satires*, Macmillan 1979.*

Garzetti, A., *From Tiberius to the Antonines*, trans. J.R. Foster, Methuen 1974.

Green, P., *Juvenal: the Sixteen Satires*, Penguin 1967. Repr. 1988.*

Highet, G., *Juvenal the Satirist*, Oxford 1954.*

Jenkyns, R.H.A., 'Juvenal the Poet', *Three Classical Poets*, London 1982, 151-221

Kennedy, G., *The Art of Rhetoric in the Roman World*, Princeton 1972.

MacMullen, R., *Roman Social Relations*, New Haven/London 1974

Mason, H.A., 'Is Juvenal a Classic?', in *Critical Essays on Roman Literature*, ed. J.P. Sullivan, Routledge 1963.

Mayor, J.E.B., *Thirteen Satires of Juvenal*, 4th edn, Macmillan 1886.

Nisbet, R.G.M., *Collected Papers on Latin Literature*, ed. S.J.Harrison, Oxford 1995, 17-28; 227-260; 272-292.

Rose, H.J., *A Handbook of Greek Mythology*, Methuen 1965.

Rudd, N., *Themes in Roman Satire*, Duckworth 1986.

——— *Juvenal: the Satires*, a verse translation with introduction and notes by W. Barr, World's Classics, Oxford 1992.

Saller, R.P., *Personal Patronage under the Early Empire*, Cambridge 1982.*

Wells, C.M., *The Roman Empire*, Fontana 1984.

Winterbottom, M., *Roman Declamation*, Bristol Classical Press 1980.

* These works have extensive bibliographies, including references to periodical literature.

SATIRE I

Semper ego auditor tantum? numquamne reponam
vexatus totiens rauci Theseide Cordi?
inpune ergo mihi recitaverit ille togatas,
hic elegos? inpune diem consumpserit ingens
5   Telephus aut summi plena iam margine libri
scriptus et in tergo necdum finitus Orestes?
nota magis nulli domus est sua quam mihi lucus
Martis et Aeoliis vicinum rupibus antrum
Vulcani; quid agant venti, quas torqueat umbras
10   Aeacus, unde alius furtivae devehat aurum
pelliculae, quantas iaculetur Monychus ornos,
Frontonis platani convolsaque marmora clamant
semper et adsiduo ruptae lectore columnae.
expectes eadem a summo minimoque poeta.
15   et nos ergo manum ferulae subduximus, et nos
consilium dedimus Sullae, privatus ut altum
dormiret. stulta est clementia, cum tot ubique
vatibus occurras, periturae parcere chartae.
       cur tamen hoc potius libeat decurrere campo,
20   per quem magnus equos Auruncae flexit alumnus,
si vacat ac placidi rationem admittitis, edam.
cum tener uxorem ducat spado, Mevia Tuscum
figat aprum et nuda teneat venabula mamma,
patricios omnis opibus cum provocet unus
25   quo tondente gravis iuveni mihi barba sonabat,
cum pars Niliacae plebis, cum verna Canopi
Crispinus Tyrias umero revocante lacernas
ventilet aestivum digitis sudantibus aurum
nec sufferre queat maioris pondera gemmae,
30   difficile est saturam non scribere. nam quis iniquae
tam patiens urbis, tam ferreus, ut teneat se,
causidici nova cum veniat lectica Mathonis
plena ipso, post hunc magni delator amici
et cito rapturus de nobilitate comesa

35   quod superest, quem Massa timet, quem munere palpat
      Carus et a trepido Thymele summissa Latino;
      cum te summoveant qui testamenta merentur
      noctibus, in caelum quos evehit optima summi
      nunc via processus, vetulae vesica beatae?
40   unciolam Proculeius habet, sed Gillo deuncem,
      partes quisque suas ad mensuram inguinis heres.
      accipiat sane mercedem sanguinis et sic
      palleat ut nudis pressit qui calcibus anguem
      aut Lugudunensem rhetor dicturus ad aram.
45   quid referam quanta siccum iecur ardeat ira,
      cum populum gregibus comitum premat hic spoliator
      pupilli prostantis et hic damnatus inani
      iudicio? quid enim salvis infamia nummis?
      exul ab octava Marius bibit et fruitur dis
50   iratis, at tu victrix, provincia, ploras.
      haec ego non credam Venusina digna lucerna?
      haec ego non agitem? sed quid magis? Heracleas
      aut Diomedeas aut mugitum labyrinthi
      et mare percussum puero fabrumque volantem,
55   cum leno accipiat moechi bona, si capiendi
      ius nullum uxori, doctus spectare lacunar,
      doctus et ad calicem vigilanti stertere naso;
      cum fas esse putet curam sperare cohortis
      qui bona donavit praesepibus et caret omni
60   maiorum censu, dum pervolat axe citato
      Flaminiam puer Automedon? nam lora tenebat
      ipse, lacernatae cum se iactaret amicae.
      nonne libet medio ceras inplere capaces
      quadrivio, cum iam sexta cervice feratur
65   hinc atque inde patens ac nuda paene cathedra
      et multum referens de Maecenate supino
      signator falsi, qui se lautum atque beatum
      exiguis tabulis et gemma fecerit uda?
      occurrit matrona potens, quae molle Calenum
70   porrectura viro miscet sitiente rubeta
      instituitque rudes melior Lucusta propinquas
      per famam et populum nigros efferre maritos.
      aude aliquid brevibus Gyaris et carcere dignum,
      si vis esse aliquid. probitas laudatur et alget;

75 criminibus debent hortos, praetoria, mensas,
    argentum vetus et stantem extra pocula caprum.
    quem patitur dormire nurus corruptor avarae,
    quem sponsae turpes et praetextatus adulter?
    si natura negat, facit indignatio versum
80 qualemcumque potest, quales ego vel Cluvienus.
       ex quo Deucalion nimbis tollentibus aequor
    navigio montem ascendit sortesque poposcit
    paulatimque anima caluerunt mollia saxa
    et maribus nudas ostendit Pyrrha puellas,
85 quidquid agunt homines, votum, timor, ira, voluptas,
    gaudia, discursus, nostri farrago libelli est.
    et quando uberior vitiorum copia? quando
    maior avaritiae patuit sinus? alea quando
    hos animos? neque enim loculis comitantibus itur
90 ad casum tabulae, posita sed luditur arca.
    proelia quanta illic dispensatore videbis
    armigero! simplexne furor sestertia centum
    perdere et horrenti tunicam non reddere servo?
    quis totidem erexit villas, quis fercula septem
95 secreto cenavit avus? nunc sportula primo
    limine parva sedet turbae rapienda togatae.
    ille tamen faciem prius inspicit et trepidat ne
    suppositus venias ac falso nomine poscas:
    agnitus accipies. iubet a praecone vocari
100 ipsos Troiugenas, nam vexant limen et illi
    nobiscum. 'da praetori, da deinde tribuno.'
    sed libertinus prior est. 'prior' inquit 'ego adsum.
    cur timeam dubitemve locum defendere, quamvis
    natus ad Euphraten, molles quod in aure fenestrae
105 arguerint, licet ipse negem? sed quinque tabernae
    quadringenta parant. quid confert purpura maior
    optandum, si Laurenti custodit in agro
    conductas Corvinus ovis, ego possideo plus
    Pallante et Licinis?' expectent ergo tribuni,
110 vincant divitiae, sacro ne cedat honori
    nuper in hanc urbem pedibus qui venerat albis,
    quandoquidem inter nos sanctissima divitiarum
    maiestas, etsi funesta Pecunia templo
    nondum habitat, nullas Nummorum ereximus aras,

115 ut colitur Pax atque Fides, Victoria, Virtus
     quaeque salutato crepitat Concordia nido.
     sed cum summus honor finito conputet anno
     sportula quid referat, quantum rationibus addat,
     quid facient comites quibus hinc toga, calceus hinc est
120 et panis fumusque domi? densissima centum
     quadrantes lectica petit, sequiturque maritum
     languida vel praegnas et circumducitur uxor.
     hic petit absenti nota iam callidus arte
     ostendens vacuam et clausam pro coniuge sellam.
125 'Galla mea est' inquit, 'citius dimitte. moraris?
     profer, Galla, caput.' 'noli vexare, quiescet.'
     ipse dies pulchro distinguitur ordine rerum:
     sportula, deinde forum iurisque peritus Apollo
     atque triumphales, inter quas ausus habere
130 nescio quis titulos Aegyptius atque Arabarches,
     cuius ad effigiem non tantum meiere fas est.
     ·
     vestibulis abeunt veteres lassique clientes
     votaque deponunt, quamquam longissima cenae
     spes homini; caulis miseris atque ignis emendus.
135 optima silvarum interea pelagique vorabit
     rex horum vacuisque toris tantum ipse iacebit.
     (nam de tot pulchris et latis orbibus et tam
     antiquis una comedunt patrimonia mensa.)
     nullus iam parasitus erit. sed quis ferat istas
     luxuriae sordes? quanta est gula quae sibi totos
     ponit apros, animal propter convivia natum!
     poena tamen praesens, cum tu deponis amictus
     turgidus et crudum pavonem in balnea portas.
     hinc subitae mortes atque intestata senectus.
145 it nova nec tristis per cunctas fabula cenas;
     ducitur iratis plaudendum funus amicis.
         nil erit ulterius quod nostris moribus addat
     posteritas, eadem facient cupientque minores,
     omne in praecipiti vitium stetit. utere velis,
150 totos pande sinus. dices hic forsitan 'unde
     ingenium par materiae? unde illa priorum
     scribendi quodcumque animo flagrante liberet
     simplicitas: "cuius non audeo dicere nomen?

quid refert dictis ignoscat Mucius an non?"?
155 pone Tigillinum, taeda lucebis in illa
qua stantes ardent qui fixo gutture fumant,
et latum media sulcum deducit harena.'
qui dedit ergo tribus patruis aconita, vehatur
pensilibus plumis atque illinc despiciat nos?
160 'cum veniet contra, digito compesce labellum:
accusator erit qui verbum dixerit "hic est."
securus licet Aenean Rutulumque ferocem
committas, nulli gravis est percussus Achilles
aut multum quaesitus Hylas urnamque secutus:
165 ense velut stricto quotiens Lucilius ardens
infremuit, rubet auditor cui frigida mens est
criminibus, tacita sudant praecordia culpa.
inde ira et lacrimae. tecum prius ergo voluta
haec animo ante tubas: galeatum sero duelli
170 paenitet.' experiar quid concedatur in illos
quorum Flaminia tegitur cinis atque Latina.

SATIRE III

Quamvis digressu veteris confusus amici
laudo tamen, vacuis quod sedem figere Cumis
destinet atque unum civem donare Sibyllae.
ianua Baiarum est et gratum litus amoeni
5 secessus. ego vel Prochytam praepono Suburae;
nam quid tam miserum, tam solum vidimus, ut non
deterius credas horrere incendia, lapsus
tectorum adsiduos ac mille pericula saevae
urbis et Augusto recitantes mense poetas?
10 sed dum tota domus raeda componitur una,
substitit ad veteres arcus madidamque Capenam.
hic, ubi nocturnae Numa constituebat amicae,
nunc sacri fontis nemus et delubra locantur
·   Iudaeis, quorum cophinus fenumque supellex
15 (omnis enim populo mercedem pendere iussa est
arbor et eiectis mendicat silva Camenis),
in vallem Egeriae descendimus et speluncas
dissimiles veris. quanto praesentius esset
numen aquis, viridi si margine cluderet undas
20 herba nec ingenuum violarent marmora tofum!
        hic tunc Umbricius 'quando artibus' inquit 'honestis
nullus in urbe locus, nulla emolumenta laborum,
res hodie minor est here quam fuit atque eadem cras
deteret exiguis aliquid, proponimus illuc
25 ire, fatigatas ubi Daedalus exuit alas,
dum nova canities, dum prima et recta senectus,
dum superest Lachesi quod torqueat et pedibus me
porto meis nullo dextram subeunte bacillo.
cedamus patria. vivant Artorius istic
30 et Catulus, maneant qui nigrum in candida vertunt,
quis facile est aedem conducere, flumina, portus,
siccandam eluviem, portandum ad busta cadaver,
et praebere caput domina venale sub hasta.
quondam hi cornicines et municipalis harenae

35 perpetui comites notaeque per oppida buccae
    munera nunc edunt et, verso pollice vulgus
    cum iubet, occidunt populariter; inde reversi
    conducunt foricas, et cur non omnia? cum sint
    quales ex humili magna ad fastigia rerum
40 extollit quotiens voluit Fortuna iocari.
    quid Romae faciam? mentiri nescio; librum,
    si malus est, nequeo laudare et poscere; motus
    astrorum ignoro; funus promittere patris
    nec volo nec possum; ranarum viscera numquam
45 inspexi; ferre ad nuptam quae mittit adulter,
    quae mandat, norunt alii; me nemo ministro
    fur erit, atque ideo nulli comes exeo tamquam
    mancus et extinctae, corpus non utile, dextrae.
    quis nunc diligitur nisi conscius et cui fervens
50 aestuat occultis animus semperque tacendis?
    nil tibi se debere putat, nil conferet umquam,
    participem qui te secreti fecit honesti.
    carus erit Verri qui Verrem tempore quo vult
    accusare potest. tanti tibi non sit opaci
55 omnis harena Tagi quodque in mare volvitur aurum
    ut somno careas ponendaque praemia sumas
    tristis et a magno semper timearis amico.
        quae nunc divitibus gens acceptissima nostris
    et quos praecipue fugiam, properabo fateri,
60 nec pudor obstabit. non possum ferre, Quirites,
    Graecam Urbem. quamvis quota portio faecis Achaei?
    iam pridem Syrus in Tiberim defluxit Orontes
    et linguam et mores et cum tibicine chordas
    obliquas nec non gentilia tympana secum
65 vexit et ad circum iussas prostare puellas.
    (ite, quibus grata est picta lupa barbara mitra.)
    rusticus ille tuus sumit trechedipna, Quirine,
    et ceromatico fert niceteria collo.
    hic alta Sicyone, ast hic Amydone relicta,
70 hic Andro, ille Samo, hic Trallibus aut Alabandis,
    Esquilias dictumque petunt a vimine collem,
    viscera magnarum domuum dominique futuri.
    ingenium velox, audacia perdita, sermo
    promptus et Isaeo torrentior. ede quid illum

75 esse putes. quemvis hominem secum attulit ad nos:
grammaticus, rhetor, geometres, pictor, aliptes,
augur, schoenobates, medicus, magus — omnia novit
Graeculus esuriens: in caelum, iusseris, ibit.
in summa non Maurus erat neque Sarmata nec Thrax
80 qui sumpsit pinnas, mediis sed natus Athenis.
horum ego non fugiam conchylia? me prior ille
signabit fultusque toro meliore recumbet,
advectus Romam quo pruna et cottana vento?
usque adeo nihil est quod nostra infantia caelum
85 hausit Aventini baca nutrita Sabina?
quid quod adulandi gens prudentissima laudat
sermonem indocti, faciem deformis amici,
et longum invalidi collum cervicibus aequat
Herculis Antaeum procul a tellure tenentis,
90 miratur vocem angustam, qua deterius nec
ille sonat quo mordetur gallina marito?
haec eadem licet et nobis laudare, sed illis
creditur. an melior cum Thaida sustinet aut cum
uxorem comoedus agit vel Dorida nullo
95 cultam palliolo? mulier nempe ipsa videtur,
non persona, loqui: vacua et plana omnia dicas
infra ventriculum et tenui distantia rima.
nec tamen Antiochus nec erit mirabilis illic
aut Stratocles aut cum molli Demetrius Haemo:
100 natio comoeda est. rides, maiore cachinno
concutitur; flet, si lacrimas conspexit amici,
nec dolet; igniculum brumae si tempore poscas,
accipit endromidem; si dixeris "aestuo," sudat.
non sumus ergo pares: melior, qui semper et omni
105 nocte dieque potest aliena sumere vultum
a facie, iactare manus laudare paratus,
si bene ructavit, si rectum minxit amicus,
si trulla inverso crepitum dedit aurea fundo.
praeterea sanctum nihil huic vel ab inguine tutum,
110 non matrona laris, non filia virgo nec ipse
sponsus levis adhuc, non filius ante pudicus.
horum si nihil est, aviam resupinat amici.
[scire volunt secreta domus atque inde timeri.]
et quoniam coepit Graecorum mentio, transi

115 gymnasia atque audi facinus maioris abollae.
Stoicus occidit Baream delator amicum
discipulumque senex ripa nutritus in illa
ad quam Gorgonei delapsa est pinna caballi.
non est Romano cuiquam locus hic, ubi regnat
120 Protogenes aliquis vel Diphilus aut Hermarchus,
qui gentis vitio numquam partitur amicum,
solus habet. nam cum facilem stillavit in aurem
exiguum de naturae patriaeque veneno,
limine summoveor, perierunt tempora longi
125 servitii; nusquam minor est iactura clientis.
    quod porro officium, ne nobis blandiar, aut quod
pauperis hic meritum, si curet nocte togatus
currere, cum praetor lictorem inpellat et ire
praecipitem iubeat dudum vigilantibus orbis,
130 ne prior Albinam et Modiam collega salutet?
divitis hic servo cludit latus ingenuorum
filius; alter enim quantum in legione tribuni
accipiunt donat Calvinae vel Catienae,
ut semel aut iterum super illam palpitet; at tu,
135 cum tibi vestiti facies scorti placet, haeres
et dubitas alta Chionen deducere sella.
da testem Romae tam sanctum quam fuit hospes
numinis Idaei, procedat vel Numa vel qui
servavit trepidam flagranti ex aede Minervam:
140 protinus ad censum, de moribus ultima fiet
quaestio. "quot pascit servos? quot possidet agri
iugera? quam multa magnaque paropside cenat?"
quantum quisque sua nummorum servat in arca,
tantum habet et fidei. iures licet et Samothracum
145 et nostrorum aras, contemnere fulmina pauper
creditur atque deos dis ignoscentibus ipsis.
quid quod materiam praebet causasque iocorum
omnibus hic idem, si foeda et scissa lacerna,
si toga sordidula est et rupta calceus alter
150 pelle patet, vel si consuto volnere crassum
atque recens linum ostendit non una cicatrix?
nil habet infelix paupertas durius in se
quam quod ridiculos homines facit. "exeat" inquit,
"si pudor est, et de pulvino surgat equestri,

155 cuius res legi non sufficit, et sedeant hic
    lenonum pueri quocumque ex fornice nati,
    hic plaudat nitidus praeconis filius inter
    pinnirapi cultos iuvenes iuvenesque lanistae."
    sic libitum vano, qui nos distinxit, Othoni.
160 quis gener hic placuit censu minor atque puellae
    sarcinulis inpar? quis pauper scribitur heres?
    quando in consilio est aedilibus? agmine facto
    debuerant olim tenues migrasse Quirites.
    haut facile emergunt quorum virtutibus obstat
165 res angusta domi, sed Romae durior illis
    conatus: magno hospitium miserabile, magno
    servorum ventres, et frugi cenula magno.
    fictilibus cenare pudet, quod turpe negabis
    translatus subito ad Marsos mensamque Sabellam
170 contentusque illic veneto duroque cucullo.
    pars magna Italiae est, si verum admittimus, in qua
    nemo togam sumit nisi mortuus. ipsa dierum
    festorum herboso colitur si quando theatro
    maiestas tandemque redit ad pulpita notum
175 exodium, cum personae pallentis hiatum
    in gremio matris formidat rusticus infans,
    aequales habitus illic similesque videbis
    orchestram et populum; clari velamen honoris
    sufficiunt tunicae summis aedilibus albae.
180 hic ultra vires habitus nitor, hic aliquid plus
    quam satis est interdum aliena sumitur arca.
    commune id vitium est: hic vivimus ambitiosa
    paupertate omnes. quid te moror? omnia Romae
    cum pretio. quid das, ut Cossum aliquando salutes,
185 ut te respiciat clauso Veiento labello?
    ille metit barbam, crinem hic deponit amati;
    plena domus libis venalibus. "accipe et istud
    fermentum tibi habe"; praestare tributa clientes
    cogimur et cultis augere peculia servis.
190   quis timet aut timuit gelida Praeneste ruinam
    aut positis nemorosa inter iuga Volsiniis aut
    simplicibus Gabiis aut proni Tiburis arce?
    nos urbem colimus tenui tibicine fultam
    magna parte sui; nam sic labentibus obstat

195 vilicus et, veteris rimae cum texit hiatum,
securos pendente iubet dormire ruina.
vivendum est illic, ubi nulla incendia, nulli
nocte metus. iam poscit aquam, iam frivola transfert
Ucalegon, tabulata tibi iam tertia fumant:
200 tu nescis; nam si gradibus trepidatur ab imis,
ultimus ardebit quem tegula sola tuetur
a pluvia, molles ubi reddunt ova columbae.
lectus erat Cordo Procula minor, urceoli sex
ornamentum abaci, nec non et parvulus infra
205 cantharus et rucubans sub eodem e marmore Chiron,
iamque vetus Graecos servabat cista libellos
et divina opici rodebant carmina mures.
nil habuit Cordus, quis enim negat? et tamen illud
perdidit infelix totum nihil. ultimus autem
210 aerumnae cumulus, quod nudum et frusta rogantem
nemo cibo, nemo hospitio tectoque iuvabit.
si magna Asturici cecidit domus, horrida mater,
pullati proceres, differt vadimonia praetor;
tum gemimus casus urbis, tunc odimus ignem.
215 ardet adhuc, et iam accurrit qui marmora donet,
conferat inpensas; hic nuda et candida signa,
hic aliquid praeclarum Euphranoris et Polycliti
aera, Asianorum vetera ornamenta deorum,
hic libros dabit et forulos mediamque Minervam,
220 hic modium argenti. meliora ac plura reponit
Persicus orborum lautissimus et merito iam
suspectus tamquam ipse suas incenderit aedes.
si potes avelli circensibus, optima Sorae
aut Fabrateriae domus aut Frusinone paratur
225 quanti nunc tenebras unum conducis in annum.
hortulus hic puteusque brevis nec reste movendus
in tenuis plantas facili diffunditur haustu.
vive bidentis amans et culti vilicus horti
unde epulum possis centum dare Pythagoreis.
230 est aliquid, quocumque loco, quocumque recessu,
unius sese dominum fecisse lacertae.
      plurimus hic aeger moritur vigilando (sed ipsum
languorem peperit cibus inperfectus et haerens
ardenti stomacho); nam quae meritoria somnum

235 admittunt? magnis opibus dormitur in Urbe.
inde caput morbi. raedarum transitus arto
vicorum in flexu et stantis convicia mandrae
eripient somnum Druso vitulisque marinis.
si vocat officium, turba cedente vehetur
240 dives et ingenti curret super ora Liburna
atque obiter leget aut scribet vel dormiet intus
(namque facit somnum clausa lectica fenestra),
ante tamen veniet: nobis properantibus obstat
unda prior, magno populus premit agmine lumbos
245 qui sequitur; ferit hic cubito, ferit assere duro
alter, at hic tignum capiti incutit, ille metretam.
pinguia crura luto, planta mox undique magna
calcor, et in digito clavus mihi militis haeret.
nonne vides quanto celebretur sportula fumo?
250 centum convivae, sequitur sua quemque culina.
Corbulo vix ferret tot vasa ingentia, tot res
inpositas capiti, quas recto vertice portat
servulus infelix et cursu ventilat ignem.
scinduntur tunicae sartae modo, longa coruscat
255 serraco veniente abies, atque altera pinum
plaustra vehunt; nutant alte populoque minantur.
nam si procubuit qui saxa Ligustica portat
axis et eversum fudit super agmina montem,
quid superest de corporibus? quis membra, quis ossa
260 invenit? obtritum volgi perit omne cadaver
more animae. domus interea secura patellas
iam lavat et bucca foculum excitat et sonat unctis
striglibus et pleno componit lintea guto.
haec inter pueros varie properantur, at ille
265 iam sedet in ripa taetrumque novicius horret
porthmea nec sperat caenosi gurgitis alnum
infelix nec habet quem porrigat ore trientem.
     respice nunc alia ac diversa pericula noctis:
quod spatium tectis sublimibus unde cerebrum
270 testa ferit, quotiens rimosa et curta fenestris
vasa cadant, quanto percussum pondere signent
et laedant silicem. possis ignavus haberi
et subiti casus inprovidus, ad cenam si
intestatus eas: adeo tot fata, quot illa

275 nocte patent vigiles te praetereunte fenestrae.
ergo optes votumque feras miserabile tecum,
ut sint contentae patulas defundere pelves.
ebrius ac petulans, qui nullum forte cecidit,
dat poenas, noctem patitur lugentis amicum
280 Pelidae, cubat in faciem, mox deinde supinus:
[ergo non aliter poterit dormire; quibusdam]
somnum rixa facit. sed quamvis inprobus annis
atque mero fervens cavet hunc quem coccina laena
vitari iubet et comitum longissimus ordo,
285 multum praeterea flammarum et aenea lampas.
me, quem luna solet deducere vel breve lumen
candelae, cuius dispenso et tempero filum,
contemnit. miserae cognosce prohoemia rixae,
si rixa est, ubi tu pulsas, ego vapulo tantum.
290 stat contra starique iubet. parere necesse est;
nam quid agas, cum te furiosus cogat et idem
fortior? "unde venis" exclamat, "cuius aceto,
cuius conche tumes? quis tecum sectile porrum
sutor et elixi vervecis labra comedit?
295 nil mihi respondes? aut dic aut accipe calcem.
ede ubi consistas: in qua te quaero proseucha?"
dicere si temptes aliquid tacitusve recedas,
tantumdem est: feriunt pariter, vadimonia deinde
irati faciunt. libertas pauperis haec est:
300 pulsatus rogat et pugnis concisus adorat
ut liceat paucis cum dentibus inde reverti.
nec tamen haec tantum metuas; nam qui spoliet te
non derit clausis domibus postquam omnis ubique
fixa catenatae siluit compago tabernae.
305 interdum et ferro subitus grassator agit rem:
armato quotiens tutae custode tenentur
et Pomptina palus et Gallinaria pinus,
sic inde huc omnes tamquam ad vivaria currunt.
qua fornace graves, qua non incude catenae?
310 maximus in vinclis ferri modus, ut timeas ne
vomer deficiat, ne marra et sarcula desint.
felices proavorum atavos, felicia dicas
saecula quae quondam sub regibus atque tribunis
viderunt uno contentam carcere Romam.

315   his alias poteram et pluris subnectere causas,
        sed iumenta vocant et sol inclinat. eundum est;
        nam mihi commota iamdudum mulio virga
        adnuit. ergo vale nostri memor, et quotiens te
        Roma tuo refici properantem reddet Aquino,
320 me quoque ad Helvinam Cererem vestramque Dianam
        converte a Cumis. saturarum ego, ni pudet illas,
        auditor gelidos veniam caligatus in agros.'

SATIRE X

Omnibus in terris, quae sunt a Gadibus usque
Auroram et Gangen, pauci dinoscere possunt
vera bona atque illis multum diversa, remota
erroris nebula. quid enim ratione timemus
5 aut cupimus? quid tam dextro pede concipis ut te
conatus non paeniteat votique peracti?
evertere domos totas optantibus ipsis
di faciles. nocitura toga, nocitura petuntur
militia; torrens dicendi copia multis
10 et sua mortifera est facundia; viribus ille
confisus periit admirandisque lacertis;
sed pluris'nimia congesta pecunia cura
strangulat et cuncta exuperans patrimonia census
quanto delphinis ballaena Britannica maior.
15 temporibus diris igitur iussuque Neronis
Longinum et magnos Senecae praedivitis hortos
clausit et egregias Lateranorum obsidet aedes
tota cohors: rarus venit in cenacula miles.
pauca licet portes argenti vascula puri
20 nocte iter ingressus, gladium contumque timebis
et mota ad lunam trepidabis harundinis umbra:
cantabit vacuus coram latrone viator.
prima fere vota et cunctis notissima templis
divitiae, crescant ut opes, ut maxima toto
25 nostra sit arca foro. sed nulla aconita bibuntur
fictilibus; tunc illa time cum pocula sumes
gemmata et lato Setinum ardebit in auro.
iamne igitur laudas quod de sapientibus alter
ridebat, quotiens a limine moverat unum
30 protuleratque pedem, flebat contrarius auctor?
sed facilis cuivis rigidi censura cachinni:
mirandum est unde ille oculis suffecerit umor.
perpetuo risu pulmonem agitare solebat
Democritus, quamquam non essent urbibus illis

35 praetextae, trabeae, fasces, lectica, tribunal.
     quid si vidisset praetorem curribus altis
     extantem et medii sublimem pulvere circi
     in tunica Iovis et pictae Sarrana ferentem
     ex umeris aulaea togae magnaeque coronae
40 tantum orbem, quanto cervix non sufficit ulla?
     quippe tenet sudans hanc publicus et, sibi consul
     ne placeat, curru servus portatur eodem.
     da nunc et volucrem, sceptro quae surgit eburno,
     illinc cornicines, hinc praecedentia longi
45 agminis officia et niveos ad frena Quirites,
     defossa in loculos quos sportula fecit amicos.
     tum quoque materiam risus invenit ad omnis
     occursus hominum, cuius prudentia monstrat
     summos posse viros et magna exempla daturos
50 vervecum in patria crassoque sub aere nasci.
     ridebat curas nec non et gaudia volgi,
     interdum et lacrimas, cum Fortunae ipse minaci
     mandaret laqueum mediumque ostenderet unguem.
      ergo supervacua aut quae perniciosa petuntur?
55 propter quae fas est genua incerare deorum?
     quosdam praecipitat subiecta potentia magnae
     invidiae, mergit longa atque insignis honorum
     pagina. descendunt statuae restemque secuntur,
     ipsas deinde rotas bigarum inpacta securis
60 caedit et inmeritis franguntur crura caballis.
     iam strident ignes, iam follibus atque caminis
     ardet adoratum populo caput et crepat ingens
     Seianus, deinde ex facie toto orbe secunda
     fiunt urceoli, pelves, sartago, matellae.
65 pone domi laurus, duc in Capitolia magnum
     cretatumque bovem: Seianus ducitur unco
     spectandus, gaudent omnes. 'quae labra, quis illi
     vultus erat! numquam, si quid mihi credis, amavi
     hunc hominem, sed quo cecidit sub crimine? quisnam
70 delator quibus indicibus, quo teste probavit?'
     'nil horum; verbosa et grandis epistula venit
     a Capreis.' 'bene habet, nil plus interrogo.' sed quid
     turba Remi? sequitur fortunam, ut semper, et odit
     damnatos. idem populus, si Nortia Tusco

75 favisset, si oppressa foret secura senectus
   principis, hac ipsa Seianum diceret hora
   Augustum. iam pridem, ex quo suffragia nulli
   vendimus, effudit curas; nam qui dabat olim
   imperium, fasces, legiones, omnia, nunc se
80 continet atque duas tantum res anxius optat,
   panem et circenses. 'perituros audio multos.'
   'nil dubium, magna est fornacula.' 'pallidulus mi
   Bruttidius meus ad Martis fuit obvius aram;
   quam timeo, victus ne poenas exigat Aiax
85 ut male defensus. curramus praecipites et,
   dum iacet in ripa, calcemus Caesaris hostem.
   sed videant servi, ne quis neget et pavidum in ius
   cervice obstricta dominum trahat.' hi sermones
   tunc de Seiano, secreta haec murmura volgi.
90 visne salutari sicut Seianus, habere
   tantundem atque illi summas donare curules,
   illum exercitibus praeponere, tutor haberi
   principis angusta Caprearum in rupe sedentis
   cum grege Chaldaeo? vis certe pila, cohortis,
95 egregios equites et castra domestica; quidni
   haec cupias? et qui nolunt occidere quemquam
   posse volunt. sed quae praeclara et prospera tanti
   ut rebus laetis par sit mensura malorum?
   huius qui trahitur praetextam sumere mavis
100 an Fidenarum Gabiorumque esse potestas
   et de mensura ius dicere, vasa minora
   frangere pannosus vacuis aedilis Ulubris?
   ergo quid optandum foret ignorasse fateris
   Seianum; nam qui nimios optabat honores
105 et nimias poscebat opes, numerosa parabat
   excelsae turris tabulata, unde altior esset
   casus et inpulsae praeceps inmane ruinae.
   quid Crassos, quid Pompeios evertit et illum
   ad sua qui domitos deduxit flagra Quirites?
110 summus nempe locus nulla non arte petitus
   magnaque numinibus vota exaudita malignis.
   ad generum Cereris sine caede ac vulnere pauci
   descendunt reges et sicca morte tyranni.
       eloquium ac famam Demosthenis aut Ciceronis

115 incipit optare et totis quinquatribus optat
    quisquis adhuc uno parcam colit asse Minervam,
    quem sequitur custos angustae vernula capsae.
    eloquio sed uterque perit orator, utrumque
    largus et exundans leto dedit ingenii fons.
120 ingenio manus est et cervix caesa, nec umquam
    sanguine causidici maduerunt rostra pusilli.
    'o fortunatam natam me consule Romam:'
    Antoni gladios potuit contemnere si sic
    omnia dixisset. ridenda poemata malo
125 quam te, conspicuae divina Philippica famae,
    volveris a prima quae proxima. saevus et illum
    exitus eripuit, quem mirabantur Athenae
    torrentem et pleni moderantem frena theatri.
    dis ille adversis genitus fatoque sinistro,
130 quem pater, ardentis massae fuligine lippus,
    a carbone et forcipibus gladiosque paranti
    incude et luteo Volcano ad rhetora misit.
        bellorum exuviae, truncis adfixa tropaeis
    lorica et fracta de casside buccula pendens
135 et curtum temone iugum victaeque triremis
    aplustre et summo tristis captivos in arcu,
    humanis maiora bonis creduntur. ad hoc se
    Romanus Graiusque et barbarus induperator
    erexit, causas discriminis atque laboris
140 inde habuit: tanto maior famae sitis est quam
    virtutis. (quis enim virtutem amplectitur ipsam,
    praemia si tollas?) patriam tamen obruit olim
    gloria paucorum et laudis titulique cupido
    haesuri saxis cinerum custodibus, ad quae
145 discutienda valent sterilis mala robora fici,
    quandoquidem data sunt ipsis quoque fata sepulcris.
    expende Hannibalem: quot libras in duce summo
    invenies? hic est quem non capit Africa Mauro
    percussa oceano Niloque admota tepenti
150 rursus ad Aethiopum populos aliosque elephantos.
    additur imperiis Hispania, Pyrenaeum
    transilit. opposuit natura Alpemque nivemque:
    diducit scopulos et montem rumpit aceto.
    iam tenet Italiam, tamen ultra pergere tendit.

155 'acti' inquit 'nihil est, nisi Poeno milite portas
    frangimus et media vexillum pono Subura.'
    o qualis facies et quali digna tabella,
    cum Gaetula ducem portaret belua luscum!
    exitus ergo quis est? o gloria! vincitur idem
160 nempe et in exilium praeceps fugit atque ibi magnus
    mirandusque cliens sedet ad praetoria regis,
    donec Bithyno libeat vigilare tyranno.
    finem animae, quae res humanas miscuit olim,
    non gladii, non saxa dabunt nec tela, sed ille
165 Cannarum vindex et tanti sanguinis ultor
    anulus. i, demens, et saevas curre per Alpes
    ut pueris placeas et declamatio fias.
    unus Pellaeo iuveni non sufficit orbis,
    aestuat infelix angusto limite mundi
170 ut Gyarae clausus scopulis parvaque Seripho;
    cum tamen a figulis munitam intraverit urbem,
    sarcophago contentus erit. mors sola fatetur
    quantula sint hominum corpuscula. creditur olim
    velificatus Athos et quidquid Graecia mendax
175 audet in historia, constratum classibus isdem
    suppositumque rotis solidum mare; credimus altos
    defecisse amnes epotaque flumina Medo
    prandente et madidis cantat quae Sostratus alis.
    ille tamen qualis rediit Salamine relicta,
180 in Corum atque Eurum solitus saevire flagellis
    barbarus Aeolio numquam hoc in carcere passos,
    ipsum conpedibus qui vinxerat Ennosigaeum
    (mitius id sane. quid? non et stigmate dignum
    credidit? huic quisquam vellet servire deorum?) –
185 sed qualis rediit? nempe una nave, cruentis
    fluctibus ac tarda per densa cadavera prora.
    has totiens optata exegit gloria poenas.
        'da spatium vitae, multos da, Iuppiter, annos.'
    hoc recto vultu, solum hoc et pallidus optas.
190 sed quam continuis et quantis longa senectus
    plena malis! deformem et taetrum ante omnia vultum
    dissimilemque sui, deformem pro cute pellem
    pendentisque genas et talis aspice rugas
    quales, umbriferos ubi pandit Thabraca saltus,

195 in vetula scalpit iam mater simia bucca.
    plurima sunt iuvenum discrimina, pulchrior ille
    hoc atque ore alio, multum hic robustior illo:
    una senum facies — cum voce trementia membra
    et iam leve caput madidique infantia nasi;
200 frangendus misero gingiva panis inermi.
    usque adeo gravis uxori natisque sibique,
    ut captatori moveat fastidia Cosso.
    non eadem vini atque cibi torpente palato
    gaudia, nam coitus iam longa oblivio, vel si
205 coneris, iacet exiguus cum ramice nervus
    et, quamvis tota palpetur nocte, iacebit.
    anne aliquid sperare potest haec inguinis aegri
    canities? quid quod merito suspecta libido est
    quae venerem adfectat sine viribus? aspice partis
210 nunc damnum alterius. nam quae cantante voluptas,
    sit licet eximius, citharoedo sive Seleuco
    et quibus aurata mos est fulgere lacerna?
    quid refert, magni sedeat qua parte theatri
    qui vix cornicines exaudiet atque tubarum
215 concentus? clamore opus est ut sentiat auris
    quem dicat venisse puer, quot nuntiet horas.
    praeterea minimus gelido iam in corpore sanguis
    febre calet sola, circumsilit agmine facto
    morborum omne genus, quorum si nomina quaeras,
220 promptius expediam quot amaverit Oppia moechos,
    quot Themison aegros autumno occiderit uno,
    quot Basilus socios, quot circumscripserit Hirrus
    pupillos, quot longa viros exorbeat uno
    Maura die, quot discipulos inclinet Hamillus;
225 percurram citius quot villas possideat nunc
    quo tondente gravis iuveni mihi barba sonabat.
    ille umero, hic lumbis, hic coxa debilis; ambos
    perdidit ille oculos et luscis invidet; huius
    pallida labra cibum accipiunt digitis alienis,
230 ipse ad conspectum cenae diducere rictum
    suetus hiat tantum ceu pullus hirundinis, ad quem
    ore volat pleno mater ieiuna. sed omni
    membrorum damno maior dementia, quae nec
    nomina servorum nec voltum agnoscit amici

235 cum quo praeterita cenavit nocte, nec illos
     quos genuit, quos eduxit. nam codice saevo
     heredes vetat esse suos, bona tota feruntur
     ad Phialen; tantum artificis valet halitus oris,
     quod steterat multis in carcere fornicis annis.
240 ut vigeant sensus animi, ducenda tamen sunt
     funera natorum, rogus aspiciendus amatae
     coniugis et fratris plenaeque sororibus urnae.
     haec data poena diu viventibus, ut renovata
     semper clade domus multis in luctibus inque
245 perpetuo maerore et nigra veste senescant.
     rex Pylius, magno si quicquam credis Homero,
     exemplum vitae fuit a cornice secundae.
     felix nimirum, qui tot per saecula mortem
     distulit atque suos iam dextra conputat annos,
250 quique novum totiens mustum bibit. oro parumper
     attendas quantum de legibus ipse queratur
     fatorum et nimio de stamine, cum videt acris
     Antilochi barbam ardentem, cum quaerit ab omni,
     quisquis adest, socio cur haec in tempora duret,
255 quod facinus dignum tam longo admiserit aevo.
     haec eadem Peleus, raptum cum luget Achillem,
     atque alius, cui fas Ithacum lugere natantem.
     incolumi Troia Priamus venisset ad umbras
     Assaraci magnis sollemnibus Hectore funus
260 portante ac reliquis fratrum cervicibus inter
     Iliadum lacrimas, ut primos edere planctus
     Cassandra inciperet scissaque Polyxena palla,
     si foret extinctus diverso tempore, quo non
     coeperat audaces Paris aedificare carinas.
265 longa dies igitur quid contulit? omnia vidit
     eversa et flammis Asiam ferroque cadentem.
     tunc miles tremulus posita tulit arma tiara
     et ruit ante aram summi Iovis ut vetulus bos,
     qui domini cultris tenue et miserabile collum
270 praebet ab ingrato iam fastiditus aratro.
     exitus ille utcumque hominis, sed torva canino
     latravit rictu quae post hunc vixerat uxor.
     festino ad nostros et regem transeo Ponti
     et Croesum, quem vox iusti facunda Solonis

275 respicere ad longae iussit spatia ultima vitae.
    exilium et carcer Minturnarumque paludes
    et mendicatus victa Carthagine panis
    hinc causas habuere; quid illo cive tulisset
    natura in terris, quid Roma, beatius umquam,
280 si circumducto captivorum agmine et omni
    bellorum pompa animam exhalasset opimam,
    cum de Teutonico vellet descendere curru?
    provida Pompeio dederat Campania febres
    optandas, sed multae urbes et publica vota
285 vicerunt; igitur Fortuna ipsius et Urbis
    servatum victo caput abstulit. hoc cruciatu
    Lentulus, hac poena caruit ceciditque Cethegus
    integer, et iacuit Catilina cadavere toto.
        formam optat modico pueris, maiore puellis
290 murmure, cum Veneris fanum videt, anxia mater
    usque ad delicias votorum. 'cur tamen' inquit
    'corripias? pulchra gaudet Latona Diana.'
    sed vetat optari faciem Lucretia qualem
    ipsa habuit; cuperes Rutilae, Verginia, gibbum
295 accipere osque tuum Rutilae dare. filius autem
    corporis egregii miseros trepidosque parentes
    semper habet: rara est adeo concordia formae
    atque pudicitiae. sanctos licet horrida mores
    tradiderit domus ac veteres imitata Sabinos,
300 praeterea castum ingenium voltumque modesto
    sanguine ferventem tribuat natura benigna
    larga manu (quid enim puero conferre potest plus
    custode et cura natura potentior omni?),
    non licet esse viro; nam prodiga corruptoris
305 improbitas ipsos audet temptare parentes:
    tanta in muneribus fiducia. nullus ephebum
    deformem saeva castravit in arce tyrannus,
    nec praetextatum rapuit Nero loripedem vel
    strumosum atque utero pariter gibboque tumentem.
310 i nunc et iuvenis specie laetare tui, quem
    maiora expectant discrimina. fiet adulter
    publicus et poenas metuet quascumque mariti
    irae debebit, nec erit felicior astro
    Martis, ut in laqueos numquam incidat. (exigit autem

315 interdum ille dolor plus quam lex ulla dolori
    concessit: necat hic ferro, secat ille cruentis
    verberibus, quosdam moechos et mugilis intrat.)
    sed tuus Endymion dilectae fiet adulter
    matronae. mox cum dederit Servilia nummos
320 fiet et illius quam non amat, exuet omnem
    corporis ornatum; quid enim ulla negaverit udis
    inguinibus ? sive est haec Oppia sive Catulla,
    deterior totos habet illic femina mores.
    'sed casto quid forma nocet?' quid profuit immo
325 Hippolyto grave propositum, quid Bellerophonti
    . . . . ?
    erubuit nempe haec ceu fastidita repulsa
    nec Stheneboea minus quam Cressa excanduit, et se
    concussere ambae. mulier saevissima tunc est
    cum stimulos odio pudor admovet. elige quidnam
330 suadendum esse putes cui nubere Caesaris uxor
    destinat. optimus hic et formonsissimus idem
    gentis patriciae rapitur miser extinguendus
    Messalinae oculis; dudum sedet illa parato
    flammeolo Tyriusque palam genialis in hortis
335 sternitur et ritu decies centena dabuntur
    antiquo, veniet cum signatoribus auspex.
    haec tu secreta et paucis commissa putabas?
    non nisi legitime volt nubere. quid placeat dic.
    ni parere velis, pereundum erit ante lucernas;
340 si scelus admittas, dabitur mora parvula, dum res
    nota Urbi et populo contingat principis aurem.
    dedecus ille domus sciet ultimus. interea tu
    obsequere imperio, si tanti vita dierum
    paucorum. quidquid levius meliusque putaris,
345 praebenda est gladio pulchra haec et candida cervix.
         nil ergo optabunt homines? si consilium vis,
    permittes ipsis expendere numinibus quid
    conveniat nobis rebusque sit utile nostris;
    nam pro iucundis aptissima quaeque dabunt di.
350 carior est illis homo quam sibi. nos animorum
    inpulsu et caeca magnaque cupidine ducti
    coniugium petimus partumque uxoris, at illis
    notum qui pueri qualisque futura sit uxor.

ut tamen et poscas aliquid voveasque sacellis
355 exta et candiduli divina tomacula porci,
orandum est ut sit mens sana in corpore sano.
fortem posce animum mortis terrore carentem,
qui spatium vitae extremum inter munera ponat
naturae, qui ferre queat quoscumque dolores,
360 nesciat irasci, cupiat nihil et potiores
Herculis aerumnas credat saevosque labores
et venere et cenis et pluma Sardanapalli.
monstro quod ipse tibi possis dare; semita certe
tranquillae per virtutem patet unica vitae.
365 nullum numen habes, si sit prudentia: nos te,
nos facimus, Fortuna, deam caeloque locamus.

SATIRE I

THEME: The writing of satire is justified.

STRUCTURE: 1–18 why I write poetry; 19–80 why I write satire; 81–146 the subject matter of satire: how the rich misuse their money and deserving clients suffer; 147–171 the need for caution.

1   *ego*: sc. *ero*.
     reponam: probably fut. indicative; retaliate.

2   *rauci*: from continual recitation.
     Cordi: an unknown epic poet.

3   *recitaverit*: probably fut. perfect.
     togatas: comedies of Roman life as distinct from *palliatae* in which setting and costume were Greek.

5-6   *Telephus . . . Orestes*: tragic heroes.
      summi libri: the end (i.e. the inside) of the papyrus roll, where there was a margin between the last column and the *umbilicus*.
      plena margine: abl. absolute; when this margin had been filled the author wrote on the back; cf. Martial 4.89.4.

7-17 *lucus Martis*: a grove of this name came into the story of the Argonauts, and also that of Cadmus.
      Aeoliis rupibus: a group of volcanic islands off the N coast of Sicily, named after the island in *Odyssey* 10.1. Aeolus, the lord of the winds, was supposed to live in Lipara or Strongyle.
      antrum Vulcani: Vulcan was connected with all the islands, but especially with Hiera.
      Aeacus: one of the three judges of the underworld, the others being Minos and Rhadamanthus.
      Monychus: a centaur who took a prominent part in the fight with the Lapiths at the wedding of Pirithous and Hippodamia. In mentioning these trite epic themes J was not thinking solely of the *Argonautica* of Valerius Flaccus (written before A.D. 93); several of the references do not fit that poem, and J's whole point is that there are many works of that kind.
      Frontonis: this may be one of Martial's patrons (*Epig.* 1.55), an

accomplished orator who was consul in A.D. 96 and dead by 117.
See Sherwin-White, *The Letters of Pliny* p. 170.
Convolsa . . . clamant . . . ruptae: a satirical version of the
'pathetic fallacy' which is common in Virgil's *Eclogues*, e.g.
Ecl. 6.10—11, 27—28, 84. *convolsus* and *ruptus* are medical terms
for wrenched limbs.
marmora: statues.
lectore: the absence of *ab* is perhaps explained by the importance
of *assiduo* which makes the phrase virtually = *assiduitate lectoris*
(W 96.1). Others would relate this to the circumstantial or
'absolute' ablative.

14   *expectes*: a jussive subjunctive of the indefinite 2nd person
          (W 126 n.2).

15   *ergo*: well then.
          subduximus: as the blow fell the schoolboy would snatch away
          his hand. Hence the dat. *ferulae* is one of 'taking away' (W 61).
          Children learnt reading, writing and arithmetic from a *litterator*
          between the ages of 7 and 11; then grammar and literature with a
          grammaticus until 15.

16   Rhetorical education proper began at the age of 16. After some
          preliminary exercises the student was taught the art of
          declamation, with its division into *suasoriae* (deliberative rhetoric)
          and *controversiae* (legal rhetoric). A speech advising Sulla to
          resign the dictatorship (which he held from 82—78 B.C.) and
          retire into private life would have been a *suasoria*. Another
          example would have been a speech advising Hannibal to attack, or
          to avoid attacking, Rome.

18   *vatibus*: a grandiose term; bards. Note the sequence *clementia . . .
          parcere . . . periturae*. The sheet of papyrus is doomed to be
          destroyed anyhow.

19   J now explains why he writes satire for preference (*potius*).

20   *magnus Auruncae alumnus*: C. Lucilius, who came from Suessa
          Aurunca on the borders of Latium and Campania. He wrote from
          about 130 to 102 B.C., and was regarded by Horace, Persius and
          Juvenal as the inventor of formal verse satire. The stately
          periphrasis and the image of the charioteer imply that he attacked
          vice in the grand heroic manner. For his fragments see *Remains
          of Old Latin* vol. 3 trans. by E. H. Warmington, Loeb Classical
          Library.

21   The mild, almost casual, tone ensures that the listener will be
          taken off guard by the tirade which follows.

22-23   *cum ... ducat ... figat* etc.: *cum* here means 'at such a time when' and so takes the subjunctive (W 234).
Mevia: this aristocratic lady is represented as dressing like an Amazon and taking part in a boar-hunt in the amphitheatre. Cf. Tacitus, *Ann.* 15.32 (under Nero) and Suetonius, *Domitian* 4.1.
venabula: poetic pl., or perhaps she had more than one spear.

24   Notice the emphasis *omnis ... unus*. The barber in question is probably Cinnamus, who was made an eques by his mistress's generosity (Martial 7.64). If so, he was in exile in Sicily by the end of A.D. 92 when Martial's seventh book appeared.

25   *gravis: graviter*. The beard was clipped between the ages of 16 and 40, after which it was shaved off. The fashion of wearing beards was revived by Hadrian. The line is a parody of Virgil, *Ecl.* 1.28.

26   *verna*: lit. 'a home-bred slave', but used as slang for 'native'.
Canopi: in fact Crispinus probably came from Memphis (Martial 7.99.2), but the decadent associations of Canopus suited J's purpose better (see Mayor on *Sat.* 15.46).

27   *Crispinus*: one should not automatically accept the description of Crispinus as 'a seller of salt fish' on the basis of *Sat.* 4.32–3. (Cf. Pope, *Epist. to Bathurst* v. 62 which speaks of Wortley Montague, a rich coal owner, as 'crying coals from street to street'.) Crispinus was doubtless a prosperous businessman, which explains how he was a prominent eques and a member of Domitian's privy council.
Tyrias: Tyre was the centre of a dyeing industry which produced expensive crimson and purple clothes. See Mayor's note.
revocante: hitching up – probably to draw attention to his cloak; the shade of Tyrian purple varied according to the light.

28   *ventilet*: waves about.
aestivum ... aurum: a gold ring for summer wear – a refinement explained in v. 29.

31   *ferreus*: unfeeling.

32   *causidici*: the word was often used with a disparaging nuance.
Mathonis: a flashy vulgarian who also appears in Martial. From *Sat.* 7.129, where he is said to be bankrupt, it appears that his litter was a piece of hollow ostentation. But we are not to know that here.

33   *plena ipso*: filled by the great man himself.

magni amici: powerful patron.
delator: if J had a particular person in mind no-one knows who
he was.

34   *et*: this connects *delator* and *rapturus*, as if J had written *qui
          detulit et rapiet.*
          comesa: as if the aristocracy were a carcase and the informer a
          vulture.

35-36   Baebius Massa was governor of Baetica in A.D. 92–93. He and
          Mettius Carus were notorious informers under Domitian; see
          Sherwin-White on Pliny 7.33.4 and 1.5.3. What a frightful
          character the *delator* must be, says J, if he is dreaded by men like
          Massa and Carus.
          Latinus: a famous mime-actor who belonged to Domitian's court
          (Suetonius, *Domitian* 15.3). To appease the *delator* he sends his
          acting partner Thymele (cf. Martial 1.4.5).

37   *summoveant*: a term used for clearing people from a magistrate's
          path; also for ousting people from a will.

38-39   *noctibus*: note the delayed position.
          in caelum etc. . the accumulation of favourable superlatives is
          is brutally destroyed by the final phrase.
          via: with the gen. means 'the road to'.
          vesica: here used coarsely to mean vulva.

40   A *hereditas* was divided into 12 *unciae*. Here Proculeius gets one
          twelfth and Gillo eleven twelfths. An *uncia*, however, was also a
          measure of length = one inch. J switches to the second meaning
          in v. 41, which presumably had some relevance to the physique
          of the two men.

41   *ad*: according to.
          partes: instead of supplying *habet* from v. 40, E.C. believes that
          partes is governed by the verbal notion implicit in *heres*.

42-44   *sanguinis*: blood is here apparently associated with semen as in
          Lucretius 4.1036 and in some other authors. But it is not easy
          to find a subject for *accipiat*, and after taking *palleat* as the effect
          of debauchery we have to change abruptly to the idea of fear.
          E.C. suggests that v. 42 should follow v. 36; the subject of
          accipiat would then be *delator*, and *sanguinis* would have its
          normal sense. Lines 37–41 would fit before the *cum* of v. 55 or
          the *cum* of v. 58. See *Bull. Inst. Class. Stud.* 13 (1966) 38.
          ut . . . anguem: a parody of *Aen.* 2.379–380.
          Lugudunensem . . . aram : an altar to Rome and Augustus was set
          up at Lyons by Drusus in 12 B.C. Caligula held a contest in

oratory there in A.D. 39-40; those who fared worst had to erase their work with their tongues or else be flogged or flung into the Rhone (Suetonius, *Caligula* 20).

45   *quid referam*: deliberative subjunctive (W 172).
        siccum: fevered.
        iecur: the liver was not uncommonly associated with anger and other emotions.

46   *hic*: this man.
        spoliator: *qui spoliavit*.

47   *prostantis*: who now has to survive by prostitution.
        hic: that man.
        damnatus: *qui damnatus est*.

48   *iudicio*: verdict.
        enim: explains *inani*; *infamia* is no punishment if the culprit keeps his ill-gotten gains.
        salvis nummis: abl. absolute.

49-50   In A.D. 100 Marius Priscus, the governor of Africa, was banished for extortion and cruelty. See Sherwin-White on Pliny 2.11–12. It is not clear how Marius avoided making reparation.
        ab octava: an hour earlier than usual.
        fruitur dis iratis: he derives profit from the gods' anger, i.e. from the disgrace which they have inflicted on him.
        victrix: in spite of your victory in court.

51   *Venusina lucerna*: Horace was born in Venusia (65 B.C.). His lamp cast the light of truth on murky places. Most editors refer to *Epist.* 2.1.112–113, where Horace says he (occasionally) wrote by lamplight. But the present context calls for a more dynamic and aggressive idea.

52–54   *non agitem*: deliberative subjunctive (W 109 n.2).
        quid magis: sc. *agitem. magis* means 'for preference'.
        Heracleas aut Diomedeas: epics about Hercules or Diomede; *agitem* is again understood.
        mugitum labyrinthi: 'the lowing of the labyrinth' refers to the minotaur, a creature which would figure in an epic on Theseus (cf. v. 2).
        puero: abl. of instrument, since Icarus is not acting voluntarily.
        fabrumque volantem: a comic periphrasis for Daedalus.

55-56   *leno*: here a compliant husband who profits from his wife's misbehaviour. J means that if a wife is entitled to benefit from the adulterer's will she does so; if she isn't her husband receives the money instead. In either case the husband and wife act in collusion. There were evidently certain circumstances in which a woman might not inherit but her husband might, e.g. if the husband had children by a previous marriage and the wife had none; or perhaps if she came under the law of Domitian against immorality (Suetonius, *Domitian* 8.3). How far the *Lex Voconia* of 169 B.C. was still in operation is not clear. (This forbade a citizen with an estate of over 100,000 sesterces to make a woman his heir.)

57   *ad calicem*: 'over his cups' (Ramsay).

58-62   The young eques who has spent his inheritance on horses expects to obtain command of a cohort – the first step in the *militia equestris*, which will eventually lead to lucrative posts in the civil service. J is not talking of betting; *praesepibus* could include the idea of racing stables (for rich young men sometimes raced on the track), but the reason actually given for his lack of money is his habit of careering up and down the highway (*dum pervolat* etc.).
          Flaminiam: the Via Flaminia went north to Ariminum.
          puer Automedon: a young version of Achilles' charioteer.
          lacernatae: the girl whom he wished to impress wore a man's cloak.

63   *ceras*: wooden surfaces covered with wax and written on with a *stilus*.

64   *iam sexta cervice*: he is now carried on the shoulders of six men, having previously had only four.

65   *patens*: exposed to view, leading to *nuda paene*.

66   *multum referens de*: recalling much of; hence 'very like'.
          supino: sprawling and indolent. The numerous passages referring to Maecenas' luxury (e.g. Seneca *Epist*. 114.4–8) are collected by Mayor.

67   *signator falsi*: the signatory of a false document. The man has altered the terms of a will in his own favour and sealed it with a counterfeit seal. Cf. Cicero, *Pro Cluentio* 41.

68   *fecerit*: subjunctive because it may be regarded as explaining in what respect the man is a criminal.
          uda: to prevent the wax from sticking to the *gemma*. The items mentioned show how little trouble is involved.

69   *Calenum*: the wine of Cales in N Campania.

70   *viro*: dat. after *porrectura*.
      sitiente: parching, cf. *sitientes aestus* in Calpurnius Siculus 5.49
      (*Minor Latin Poets*, Loeb, p. 262). The ancients believed that
      toads were poisonous. They have in fact venomous glands, but
      the poison would not be lethal to humans.

71   *melior Lucusta*: a superior Lucusta. This woman was employed
      by Agrippina to murder Claudius (Tacitus *Ann.* 12.66) and by
      Nero to murder Britannicus. She also took pupils (Suetonius,
      Nero 33.3).

72   *per famam et populum*: surrounded by scandal and the people;
      an instance of zeugma.
      nigros: as a result of poison.
      efferre: escort to burial; the widow would not literally shoulder
      the bier.

73   *Gyaris*: here a neuter pl., though feminine sing. in 10.170. It is a
      barren little island in the Cyclades to which criminals were
      banished.
      carcere: this implies execution. Convicts were kept in prison only
      until the next stage of their sentence could be carried out.

74   *et*: to translate 'and yet' ruins the ironic effect.

75   *criminibus*: crimes.
      hortos: parks
      praetoria: mansions.
      mensas: 'tables' not 'meals' in view of what follows. A favourite
      kind was made of citrus wood with an ivory stand. See Mayor
      on v. 137 of this satire.

76   *et*: including.
      caprum: the usual explanation is that the goat is embossed in
      high relief so that it stands on the outside of the cup. But it is
      more dramatically effective to think of the goat providing the
      handle; the animal is upright with its front hooves on the rim;
      see J. G. Griffith, *Greece and Rome* 20 (1973) 79–80.

77   *corruptor*: the man who seduces his own daughter-in-law with the
      aid of money. The addition of *avarae* makes both partners equally
      culpable.

78   *sponsae turpes*: girls, even as young as 12 or 13, who betray their
      fiancés.
      praetextatus: still wearing the purple-bordered *toga praetexta*;
      i.e. under 16.

79-80   The first line is a general statement: if nature refuses, indignation
          creates poetry. J then continues: in so far as it can — of the type
          written by myself or Cluvienus.
          Cluvienus: an unknown and, by implication, a third-rate satirist.

80-86   The construction is *quidquid agunt homines ex quo Deucalion
          ascendit*, i.e. 'whatever men *have been doing* since . . .;' *agunt* is
          present tense because such activities are still going on.
          Deucalion: the story of how Deucalion and Pyrrha survived the
          flood and restored the human race by throwing stones over their
          shoulders in told in Ovid, *Met.* 1.318–415.
          navigio montem ascendit: climbed the mountain (i.e. Mt.
          Parnassus) in a boat. v. 83 is a beautiful line based on Ovid, *Met.*
          1.400–401; *mollia* is proleptic: the stones grew warm, becoming
          soft. Then the effect is characteristically ruined by v. 84 which
          pictures Pyrrha as the madam of a brothel.
          maribus: from *mas*.
          discursus: dashing about.
          farrago: mixed fodder for cattle; hence mish-mash. The word is
          no doubt meant to recall the original meaning of *satura*, which
          was an edible mixture, whether a dish of first fruits or the filling
          of a sausage.
          libelli: Book 1, which comprised satires 1–5.

87   *et*: introduces an indignant question. J now makes it clear that by
          votum, timor etc. he means foolish and discreditable forms of
          those activities.

88   *maior*: used predicatively (W 88 n.). English would probably use
          a slightly different idiom: 'when did Greed's pocket gape so
          wide?'
          sinus: the fold at the top of the toga was used as a pocket.

89   *hos animos*: there are a few other cases of this ellipse. Here it is
          best to understand a verb meaning 'cause' or 'produce' (e.g.
          dedit), as in Seneca, *Troades* 339, rather than a verb meaning
          'assume' (e.g. *sumpsit*). Translate 'when did dice ever cause such
          mad excitement?'.

90   Instead of a small cash-box (*loculus*) the gambler has his chest
          beside him; *posita* is parallel to *comitantibus*.

91-92   *dispensatore . . . armigero*: with the steward in the role of the
          squire.
          simplexne furor: the behaviour described is not simple but double
          madness, because to the madness of the spendthrift is added that
          of the miser. Others take it to mean 'is it simply madness and not
          something else too?'

sestertia: a *sestertium* was a sum of 1,000 sesterces.

93   *reddere*: not 'restore' but 'give', implying that the slave has a right
       to decent clothing.

94   *quis*: sc. *avus*.
       fercula septem: an inordinate number; three were considered
       ample.

95-96 *secreto*: adv.
       sportula: originally a small basket of food which a client might
       receive as a substitute for a dinner; but by now it has been
       converted into a sum of money – usually 25 asses.
       primo limine: i.e. in the front porch, cf. v. 132.
       turbae rapienda togatae: the first two words destroy the dignity of
       the third.

97   *ille*: the man – probably the *dispensator* of 91. The patron
       himself would hardly have performed so lowly a duty.

99   *agnitus*: only when recognized.
       praecone: a clerk with a register who calls out the names.

100   *Troiugenas*: ironically referring to the old families who claimed
       some connection with Troy. In the late republic Varro had
       compiled a list of such families.

102   *adsum*: I was here.

104   *molles*: this connoted effeminacy and decadence.
       fenestrae: holes for ear-rings.

105   *arguerint*: potential subjunctive (W 119).

106   *quadringenta parant*: provide me with a fortune (not an income)
       of 400 (sc. *sestertia*: sums of 1,000 sesterces). 400,000 sesterces
       was the property qualification of an eques. This is here alleged to
       be just as good as senatorial status, which was signified by a
       broad purple stripe down the front of the tunic, as distinct from
       the narrow stripe of the equites. The senatorial census was 1
       million sesterces, but certain families had fallen on hard times
       and could not retain their position without assistance.

107   *Laurenti*: adjective (nom. *Laurens*). The Laurentine district was
       on the coast of Latium. Pliny had property there on which he
       kept many flocks of sheep (*Epist.* 2.17.3).

108   *Corvinus*: M. Valerius Messalla Corvinus, cos. A.D. 58, who was

granted a yearly pension of 500,000 sesterces by Nero to enable him to keep up appearances (Tacitus, *Ann.* 13.34). J represents him as making a living by hiring someone else's sheep − i.e. leasing the flock, looking after it, and sharing the profit with the owner (*locator*).

109   *Pallante et Licinis*: Pallas was a freedman who as Claudius' treasurer made a fortune of 300 million sesterces; Licinus was a Gallic prisoner of Julius Caesar who was emancipated by Augustus and later acquired enormous wealth as procurator of Gaul (16−15 B.C.). The pl. is generic: men like Licinus.

110   *sacro honori*: tribunes were traditionally regarded as sacrosanct, and in the republic they had possessed real power. To judge from Pliny 1.23 they were still treated in some quarters with a certain degree of respect, but it is clear that J exaggerates their status in order to denigrate the upstart. The power of wealth is now *sanctissima* (112).

111   *pedibus albis*: in the slave-market chalk was put on the feet of imported slaves to distinguish them from *vernae*.
        venerat: not distinguishable from an aorist (GL 241 n.1).

115   *atque*: the word carries no great force, but Postgate's *Fama* (*Class. Quart.* 3 p. 67), which is based on the manuscript R's *firma*, cannot be accepted in the absence of satisfactory evidence for such a cult.

116   Concordia who clatters when her nest is saluted (by passers by), the deity being humorously conflated with the stork which has nested on the temple roof. The main temple of Concord was at the edge of the forum at the bottom of the Capitol.

117   *summus honor*: a consul.

118   *rationibus*: lit. 'accounts', here income.
        addat: the subject is *sportula*.

119   *hinc*: from the sum provided by the *sportula*.

120-121 *fumus*: lit. 'smoke', hence 'firewood'.
        centum quadrantes: 100 quarters, 25 asses, 6¼ sesterces.

122   *circumducitur*: she attends more than one *salutatio*.

123   *nota iam callidus arte*: 'who is now an expert at the well-known trick'. Because he *is* an expert, he gets away with it.

124   *clausam*: the curtains are drawn.

125   *citius dimitte*: 'don't keep her too long'.

126   *noli vexare, quiescet*: 'don't disturb her; she'll be asleep.' When
       these words are given to the deluded *dispensator*, the trick is
       shown to be successful and the little scene is nicely rounded off.
       For the future indicating likelihood see GL 242 n.2.

127   A grand line – deflated by *sportula* in v. 128.

128   *forum*: business began about 8 a.m.
       Apollo: in the *forum Augusti* (completed in 12 B.C.) stood an
       ivory statue of Apollo. He is learned in law because he has been at
       the centre of legal business for so long.

129   *triumphales*: sc. *statuae*. In the two semi-circular porticoes on
       either side of the temple of Mars Ultor in the *forum Augusti* the
       emperor Augustus set up statues of the great Roman generals in
       in triumphant robes; others were added later.

130   *titulos*: honorific inscriptions on the base of a statue giving the
       man's name and details of his career.
       Aegyptius atque Arabarches: J is referring to Tiberius Julius
       Alexander, who came from a wealthy Jewish family but
       abandoned the faith and in return for his services to Vespasian
       eventually became Prefect of Egypt. His triumphal statue was
       presumably a recognition of his part in the Jewish campaigns of
       Titus A.D. 70.
       Arabarches: a high-up customs official, but here used contempt-
       uously: 'some Egyptian tax-wallah.'

131   *non tantum meiiere*: understand *sed etiam cacare*. Statues often
       carried notices forbidding such defilement. In referring to
       Alexander's statue J appears to be using *fas* in the sense of
       'morally permissible' as distinct from 'legally permissible'; cf.
       10.257.

132   It is clear that between v. 131 and v. 132 some lines have dropped
       out which followed the course of the day's events and brought
       the clients with their patron back from the forum to the
       vestibula. So Housman.
       veteres: of long standing.

133   *vota deponunt*: abandon hope.

134   Instead of being fed and warmed in the rich man's house they
       have to buy a cabbage and some fuel.

136   *rex*: frequently used of a patron, usually without irony; cf.
        Horace, *Epist.* 1.7.37.

137   *orbibus*: tables made from horizontal sections of a tree were
        called *orbes.*

138   *mensa*: i.e. they need only one of their numerous tables for their
        expensive meals.

139   Soon parasites will be extinct. Does this remark enforce or
        weaken J's attack on gluttons?

140   *luxuriae sordes*: an oxymoron: extravagant meanness. The
        genitive is possessive ('the meanness that belongs to self-
        indulgence').

141   *propter*: for the purpose of.

143   *crudum*: undigested. There is a good deal to be said, however,
        for reading *crudus . . . portans.* Cf. Horace, *Epist.* 1.6.61 and see
        E.C. in *Bull. Inst. Class. Stud.* 13 (1966) 38.

144   *intestata*: this reading, given by all the MSS, has caused much
        controversy. If correct, it has nothing to do with wills; for it
        would be nonsensical to say 'as a result of gluttony and a hot
        bath comes sudden death and an old age without a will'. A clue
        is perhaps provided by Martial 6.29.7: *immodicis brevis est aetas
        et rara senectus* – 'the extravagantly gifted have a short life and
        rarely reach old age'. If for *rara* we substitute the more exag-
        gerated *intestata* in the sense of 'unattested' and then turn back
        to Juvenal we get 'as a result comes sudden death and unattested
        old age'; i.e. in the case of a glutton old age is unheard of – there
        are no examples. This was Housman's view, see *Class. Rev.* 13
        (1899) 432–434. It is true that *intestatus* appears nowhere else in
        this sense, but Pomponius (writing at the start of the first century
        B.C.) has *ipsus cum uno servo senex intestato proficiscitur* –
        'The old man himself sets out unobserved with a single slave'
        (*com.* 113). This is the solution favoured by N.R. E.C., however,
        is not satisfied that the passage of Pomponius warrants such a
        use of *intestata* and so he would prefer to print provisionally (in
        the absence of a better conjecture) Corelli's *intemptata*
        'unachieved', which when written as *intentata* could have been
        corrupted to *intestata*: see *Class. Rev.* 19 (1905) 305.

146   *plaudendum*: the corpse, which would normally have been
        plangendum, provokes cheers from the 'friends' who are angry
        because they have not been invited to the rich man's dinner-
        table.

147   *addat*: for the subjunctive see GL 631.2.

149   *in praecipiti stetit*: has stopped at a precipice; i.e. it can't go any
        farther.
        utere: imperative; J exhorts himself to use all the resources of the
        grand style.

150-151 Where are you going to find a talent commensurate with the
        subject?
        materiae unde: note the hiatus after the first syllable of the
        fourth foot. There are only two other examples in J (2.26 and
        5.158); they too are assisted by a sense pause. There are eight
        cases of hiatus after the first syllable of the third foot, and one
        (12.36) after the first syllable of the second.
        priorum: 'forefathers', or perhaps more specifically 'predecessors'.

152   *scribendi*: the genitive defines *simplicitas* (153); see W 72.5.
        liberet: for the generalizing subjunctive see W 196, GL 567 n.

153-154 *cuius . . . non*: these two questions illustrate what J means by
        'our forefathers' outspokenness'. The allusion to the practice of
        naming contemporaries and the explicit reference to Mucius show
        that the speaker is using Lucilius as a mouthpiece. We should not
        assume, however, that the words are an actual quotation; Lucilius
        would not have shortened the *o* of *audeo*.
        Mucius: either 1. P. Mucius Scaevola cos. 133 B.C., a vigorous
        opponent of Lucilius' patron Scipio Aemilianus (he does not,
        however, actually figure in the fragments) or 2. Q. Mucius
        Scaevola cos. 117 B.C. who does figure in the fragments of Book
        2. (There is no evidence, however, that he was attacked in the
        manner implied here and in Persius 1.115.)

115-157 *pone*: portray.
        Tigillinum: the favourite of Nero who became *praefectus
        praetorio* in A.D. 62 and who directed the persecution of the
        Christians on the charge of arson in A.D. 64. For details of his
        appalling career see Mayor's note.
        taeda . . . harena: 'you will shine as part of that torch in which
        those who are fastened by the throat stand smoking and burning,
        and which makes a broad track across the middle of the arena.'
        According to this explanation the victims are wrapped in pitch-
        covered garments and then fastened to a row of stakes. When set
        on fire they make a broad track of flame. This view is favoured
        by N.R. (It seems unnecessary, however, to suppose that J's
        phrasing is a reminiscence of *Aen.* 2.697–698.)

        E.C. prefers the explanation offered by Housman which assumes
        the loss of a line after v. 156. The lost line will have been some-

thing like *quorum informe unco trahitur post fata cadaver* –
'whose hideous corpse is dragged after death by a hook'. *cadaver*
will then be the subject of *deducit*. In either case J is referring to
the atrocities recorded by Tacitus, *Ann.* 15.44.

158-159 Shall evil, then, be allowed to pass without protest?
tribus patruis: the Roman uncle (unlike ours) was an unpopular
figure; cf. *ne sis patruus mihi* (Horace, *Sat.* 2.3.88).
vehatur . . . despiciat: deliberative subjunctives in an indignant
question (W 109 n.2).
pensilibus plumis: the down cushions are seen from underneath as
the litter passes overhead; see *OLD pensilis*, sense 3.

161   Even the remark (*verbum*) 'that's the man' will be interpreted as
an accusation.

162-164 *securus*: without fear.
committas: pit Aeneas against Turnus, i.e. write an epic like
Virgil's.
nulli gravis est: 'no one is offended by', or possibly 'no one is
endangered by'.
percussus Achilles: the slaughter of Achilles in an epic like the
Aethiopis; see *Ox. Class. Dict.* under Epic Cycle 4.8. Statius
wrote an (incomplete) *Achilleis* under Domitian.
Hylas: the boy who accompanied Hercules on the Argonautic
expedition. At Cius on the Propontis he went to fetch water
but was pulled into the spring by the nymphs. He was sought in
vain by Hercules (*multum quaesitus*). See Apollonius 1.1177ff.,
Theocritus, *Idyll* 13, and Propertius 1.20. Virgil, *Georg.* 3.6
(*cui non dictus Hylas puer?*) shows that the subject was well worn.
urnamque secutus: a comic phrase. These references to trite and
irrelevant mythological themes provide a framework for the
defence of satire; cf. 1–14 above.

165-170 Granted, Lucilius was a fearless critic, but that kind of thing is
dangerous. So draw back while there is still time.
quotiens infremuit: for the perfect tense in iterative action see
GL 567; English translates with a present.
frigida: the chill of fear.
criminibus: abl. of cause; crimes.
praecordia: a physiological term, but sometimes used as here for
conscience.
inde: that is the cause of. The *tubae* gave the signal for battle.
Roman soldiers did not put on their helmets until battle was
imminent.
duelli: an archaic word which underlines the solemnity of the
warning.

170-171 I shall see what is legally permissible against the dead.
    Flaminia . . . Latina: the first ran north to Ariminum, the second
    south to Beneventum, passing through Aquinum, J's home town.
    Burial within the city was normally forbidden. Tombs were set
    alongside the main roads so that passers by might read the
    inscriptions.

QUESTION FOR DISCUSSION

Does J's arrangement of the subject matter form any discernible pattern?

SUGGESTED EXERCISES

1.   Examine the theme of retaliation in vv. 1–18.

2.   In vv. 22–80 how often can you find the sequence: 'when a, b,
and c are happening then I must write satire'?

3.   Compare the strategy of the satire as a whole with that of Horace,
Sat. 2.1 and Persius 1.

4.   How many instances can you find of things being treated as
persons and persons as things? What is the effect of this device?

FURTHER READING

J. Carcopino, *Daily Life in Ancient Rome*, Pelican 1956.
E. Courtney, 'Some Thought Patterns in Juvenal', *Hermathena* 118 (1974) 15-21.
J. G. Griffith, 'The Ending of Juvenal's First Satire and Lucilius, Book 30', *Hermes* 98
        (1970) 56-72.
E. J. Kenney, 'The First Satire of Juvenal', *Proc. Camb. Philol. Soc.* 8 (1962) 29-40.

SATIRE III

THEME: Life in Rome has become intolerable.

STRUCTURE: 1–20 introduction; 21–189 the difficulty of making a living (21–57 the penalties of honesty; 58–125 the penalties of being a Roman citizen rather than a Greek or oriental immigrant; 126–189 the penalties of poverty); 190–314 the discomforts and dangers of the city (190–231 falling buildings and fires; 232–267 crowds and traffic; 268–314 perils of the night, accidents, and assaults); 315–322 epilogue.

The introduction foreshadows the main topics of the satire, and the epilogue recalls several features of the introduction.

1   *confusus*: upset.

2-3   *Cumis*: Cumae, 12 miles W of Naples, was founded by the Greeks c. 750 B.C. It was a powerful city in the 7th and 6th centuries, but suffered from Etruscan and Samnite attacks in the 5th. Although famous for its temple of Apollo and the oracular Sibyl, it was later overshadowed by Puteoli, which was founded as a colony in 194 B.C. The adjective *vacuis* is first taken to mean no more than 'quiet' – cf. Horace, *Epist*. 1.7.45 and 2.2.81. But the next line compels us to think of the place as literally empty – a ghost town.

4-5   *ianua Baiarum*: Cumae was 'the gateway to Baiae', the fashionable resort 6 miles S along the peninsula.
        amoeni secessus: gen. of quality (W 84–85) co-ordinate though not connected with *gratum*.
        Prochytam: Prochyta was a small desolate island off Misenum, and so even farther than Cumae from Rome.
        Suburae: the Subura, between the Esquiline and the Viminal, was one of the busiest and most disreputable streets in Rome.

7   *credas*: because of the indefinite second person this would be subjunctive even if it were not in a result clause.
        incendia etc.: see the works by Carcopino (chap. 2) and Yavetz below.
        saevae: a word appropriate to wild and savage nature, here tellingly combined with *urbis*.

51

9   *Augusto mense*: the heat made the recitations even more unbear-
         able. Nevertheless the bathos is unmistakable.

10   Wagons were not allowed in the city by day; so Umbricius' effects
         were to be taken to the gate and loaded there. Note the emphasis
         of *tota . . . una*.

11   *veteres arcus madidamque Capenam*: hendiadys. An aqueduct
         passed over the arch. The Via Appia left Rome through the Porta
         Capena and led south to Capua.

12-17   There are two *ubi* clauses, viz. *ubi Numa constituebat* (*sed*) *nunc
         nemus et delubra locantur*; then a relative clause *quorum . . .
         supellex*; then a parenthesis *omnis . . . Camenis*; then the main
         clause *hic . . . in vallem descendimus*. King Numa is supposed to
         have learnt his laws from the nymph Egeria, whom Livy (1.21.3)
         refers to as his *coniunx*; J speaks of him as 'dating his girl-friend'.
         delubra: poetic pl., the shrine of the nymphs.
         cophinus fenumque: probably a hay-box, which would provide a
         hot meal on the Sabbath when cooking was forbidden. Jewish
         refugees had made their way to Rome in increasing numbers after
         the sack of Jerusalem in A.D. 70. J's words imply that in return
         for payment they have been allowed to occupy the grove and
         whatever structure was associated with Egeria and the nymphs; he
         elaborates on this by claiming that every tree has to pay rent to
         the people (suggesting, presumably, that every piece of ground
         inside the grove has a shack or lean-to whose occupants are
         charged rent by the city authorities); to pay this rent the wood
         has to beg (i.e. passers by are accosted by beggars and peddlars).
         It is hard to know how literally we should take all this. E.C.
         thinks J is referring not to actual rent but to the special tax which
         all Jews had to pay.

17-20   *speluncas*: the principal grotto was that of Egeria. Such places,
         says J, are no longer in their natural state; both they and their
         surroundings have been tastelessly embellished with imported
         marble.
         numen: a spirit of mystery which evokes respect.

21-22   *Umbricius*: although Umbricius may well be a fictitious character,
         inscriptions with the name have been found at Puteoli (*CIL*
         10.3141–3142). If he is fictitious, why did J choose the name?
         One can only guess; 'the shadow of old Rome' seems less likely
         than 'the man seeking shelter and rest.'
         artibus honestis . . . laborum: it becomes clear that Umbricius
         means not ordinary work but genteel occupations.

23-24   We are still in a *quando* clause. *eadem* goes with *res*: 'and tomorrow it will also have something rubbed off the little that remains.' For other, somewhat easier, expressions of the same kind see Housman on Manilius 1.539 and *Class. Quart.* 27 (1933) 4. With the present text *cras* cannot be the subject; nor can it easily be made the subject by emendation, for when used as a noun *cras* elsewhere has an adjective, e.g. Persius 5.68.

25   A satirical use of periphrasis; for Daedalus at Cumae, cf. *Aen.* 6.14ff.

26   *prima senectus*: the period between the ages of 45 and 60.

27   *Lachesi*: dat. Lachesis was one of the three Parcae, the others being Clotho and Atropos.

29-30   *patria*: native place. Nothing is known of Artorius or Catulus.

31-40   These lines convey the attitude of a man with a smallish unearned income, who regards such business activities as beneath him and who despises (and envies) those who profit from them.

31-33   That is, 'those who are ready to undertake the building or repair of temples, the dredging or embanking of rivers, the construction or clearing of harbours, the draining of flooded areas, the carrying out of the dead to burial'.
        quis: dat.
        siccandam eluviem: this is unlikely to mean cleaning out a sewer, for which *purgare* would be a more suitable verb.
        praebere caput venale: 'to offer their head for sale' means 'to make a fraudulent bankruptcy'. J speaks figuratively, as if the man had himself sold up rather than his property; cf. Cicero, *Pro Sest.* 57; *De domo* 52; and Seneca *De ira* 1.2.1. A spear was set up at public auctions, which were originally established to sell the spoils of war. *domina hasta* is the spear which confers ownership.

34-36   Men who once toured the country towns as horn players with a company of gladiators are now rich enough to present shows of their own; cf. Tacitus, *Ann.* 4.62; 15.34.
        verso pollice: the unfavourable sign was apparently, thumbs up (Apuleius, *Met.* 2.21) and the favourable sign thumbs down (Pliny *NH* 28.25).
        occidunt: by giving the order.

38   *conducunt foricas*: they undertake the latrine business; i.e. the *conductor* pays a lump sum to the *locator* and then makes his profit from the small admission charge and from the sale of excrement to manure merchants.
        cur non omnia: sc. *faciant*.

42-44   As I am no astrologer I cannot please an heir by promising the
         early death of his father.
         ranarum viscera: the verb *inspexi* points to divination rather than
         to poisoning or magic spells.

47   The assumption is that governors expect their staff (*comites*) to
         aid and abet them in extortion.

48   *corpus non utile*: in apposition to the subject.
         mancus et extinctae ... dextrae: adjective plus gen. of quality.
         His honesty makes him unfit for service.

49   *cui*: two short syllables.

50   *occultis ... tacendis*: neuter nouns.

52-53   *secreti*: a noun. The emphasis falls on *honesti*. This is followed in
         adversative asyndeton (i.e. contrast without connection) by a
         reference to Verres, the notorious governor of Sicily (73-71
         B.C.) who was prosecuted by Cicero.

54-55   *tanti*: gen. of value.
         non sit: the *non* suggests that this is a potential rather than a
         jussive subjunctive.
         harena ... quodque ... aurum: hendiadys for '(literally) golden
         sand'. The Tagus, flowing west across the middle of Spain, had
         gold deposits.
         opaci: shaded by foliage. The adjective suggests a visual contrast
         between golden sand and dark green leaves; cf. *Aen*. 6.204.

56   *ponenda*: because 'you can't take it with you'.

57   *tristis*: probably goes with *sumas;* 'gloomily accept gifts which
         you will eventually have to give up'.
         amico: patron.

60-61   *Quirites*: the name of the Romans as a civic community, which
         went back to their early union with the Sabines. (The name
         Quirites was supposed to have referred originally to those who
         came from the Sabine town of Cures.) Here the name is tellingly
         set beside *Graecam*, an adjective applied generally to people who
         spoke Greek. *Graecam Urbem* virtually means 'a Greek Rome'.

61   *quamvis*: and yet; Cicero would have used *quamquam*.
         Achaei: nom. pl.; people from the Roman province of Achaea
         which covered the Greek peninsula S of Thessaly. 'What fraction
         of the rabble is from Greece proper?'

62   *Orontes*: Antioch's river. J implies that the orientals are so much
        refuse carried down by the stream.

63-65   *linguam*: Greek *koine*.
        chordas obliquas: oriental harps, like the *sambuca*.
        gentilia: belonging to their race.
        tympana: tambourines.
        iussas: the fact that the girls act under compulsion does not make
        them less contemptible to J.

66   *ite*: sc. *ad circum*.
        picta mitra: a bright embroidered Phrygian bonnet with the apex
        folded towards the front.

67   *trechedipna*: 'dinner runners'; light shoes or sandals, possibly
        associated with comic parasites.

68   *niceteria*: medals.
        ceromatico collo: the devotee of the wrestling school leaves
        smudges of *ceroma* on his neck. These, along with the medals, are
        signs of his hobby. *ceroma* was a special mud surface used in the
        wrestling school. See O. W. Reinmuth, *Phoenix* 21 (1967),
        191–195.

69-70   *Sicyon*: 12 miles W of Corinth.
        Amydon: in Macedonia.
        Andros and Samos: islands in the Aegean.
        Tralles and Alabanda: cities in Caria, both provincial assize
        centres. Note the hiatus at the strong caesura in v. 70.

71   *Esquilias*: a wealthy district.
        dictum a vimine collem: this grandiose periphrasis does duty for
        Viminalem, which is unmetrical.

72   *viscera*: vital organs; cf. Lucan 7.579.

73   *audacia perdita*: shameless impudence.

74   *Isaeo*: i.e. *Isaei sermone* – a common type of short-cut. Isaeus
        was an Assyrian rhetorician who made a great impression when he
        came to Rome about A.D. 97. Cf. Pliny, *Epist.* 2.3.

76   *geometres*: a surveyor or perhaps a teacher of geometry. In spite
        of the omega in Greek the word should probably be scanned with
        a short o, as in Sidonius Apollinaris, *Epist.* 4.11.9. and *Carm.*
        23.114. J. does not employ synizesis, which would run the *e* into
        the *o* and allow the *o* to remain long.
        aliptes: masseur, trainer.

77   *magus*: sorcerer.

78   *Graeculus*: a contemptuous diminutive.
        in caelum, iusseris, ibit: *iusseris* is perfect subjunctive: order and
        he will go.

79   *in summa*: in fact. So P. T. Stevens, *Class. Rev.* 63 (1949) 91.
        Sarmata: nom. sing. masc. The Sarmatians lived between the
        Vistula and the Don.

80   The man referred to is Daedalus. *sumere pinnas* meant 'to grow
        wings'; cf. 14.76.

81   *conchylia*: purple clothes. The dye was extracted from a shellfish;
        see Mayor on 1.27.

82   Romans invited their friends in order of precedence to witness
        marriage-contracts, wills, and other documents.
        toro meliore: a higher place at table.

83   The immigrant is thought of as a piece of cargo.

84   *caelum*: air.

85   *hausit*: drew in, breathed.
        baca Sabina: i.e. the olive.

86   *quid quod*: what of the further fact that . . .? *prudens*, like
        peritus, was often used with the gen. (GL 374 n:4).

87   *indocti*: sc. *amici* (patron).

88   *cervicibus*: the pl. is often used in the same sense as the sing. The
        distinction here between *cervices* and *collum* (if there is one) is
        hard to define; cf. Quintilian 11.3.82.

89   *Antaeus*: this African giant was invincible as long as he remained
        in contact with his mother earth. Hercules held him off the
        ground and strangled him (Ovid, *Met.* 9.183–184). J seems to
        have in mind a work of art. Cf. Philostratus, *Imagines* 2.21, and
        the statue by Pollaiuolo.

90-91   *angustam*: squeaky, as opposed to full-throated.
        nec: not even. The full construction would have been: *qua
        deterius sonat ne mariti quidem vox illius quo mordetur gallina.*
        The cock holds the hen by the crest when mating. A double
        entendre is suggested between *gallus* 'cock' and *Gallus* 'eunuch
        priest'.

93-99   Is any actor better (than the Greek) when he plays Thais (i.e. the
        courtesan) or the wife (i.e. the lady of the house) or Doris (i.e.
        the servant girl who wears only her tunic)? Why (*nempe*) the
        woman herself, not a performer, seems to be speaking . . . yet
        (*tamen*) even famous actors are not remarkable in Greece,
        because everyone is an actor there.
        Thaida: a dactyl; the ending is that of a Greek acc.
        dicas: potential subjunctive (W 118).
        distantia: divided. The names belong to well-known actors; cf.
        Quintilian 11.3.178.

100-103 *rides*: a paratactic construction; cf. v. 78 above. In view of the
        indefinite subject the subjunctive would have been more normal;
        cf. *poscas* (102).
        conspexit: this is a 'present general' type of condition (W 193
        and 194b).
        poscas: this is another 'present general' type (W 193 and 197),
        not future ideal.
        dixeris: perfect subjunctive with an indefinite subject. For
        variety and convenience J takes full advantage of the flexibility
        of the Latin conditional. English would use the same construction
        throughout: 'he weeps if he sees'.
        cachinno concutitur: note the cackling effect.
        igniculum: brazier.
        endromidem: a heavy woollen wrap having the function of a
        sweater or track-suit.

104   *melior* (*est*): he always wins.

106   *iactare manus*: a gesture of admiration. *iactare* and *laudare* both
        go with *paratus*.

107   *ructare*: belching, at least in male company, was not forbidden
        by Roman etiquette.

108   Lit. 'if the golden *trulla* with its bottom upside down has made a
        noise'. No interpretation has won general acceptance. Is the
        trulla a drinking cup which gurgles when emptied, a commode
        with an inverted bottom, or a basin at which the guests urinate?
        The first idea, which might refer to a special kind of cup (Athen-
        aeus 6.262b) provides a feeble anti-climax; the second (preferred
        by N.R.) is rhetorically apt, but the device envisaged is not
        properly attested; the third does not square with the other
        routine and commonplace activities (*ructare* and *mingere*) and
        seems more suited to an undergraduate celebration.

109   The best manuscript (P) reads *nihil ab inguine*, which is defective
        in sense and metre. Housman proposed *nihil aut tibi*, but J

provides no other example of elision at a trochaic caesura in the fourth foot. Developing an idea of Jacoby's, Green suggests *nihil huic vel ab inguine*. The line will then mean: moreover, nothing is sacred to this man or safe from his penis.

112   *horum si nihil est*: failing these; cf. 6.331.

113   Many scholars since Housman have regarded this as a gloss inserted by a scribe to explain the odd behaviour of the Greek in v.112. A few (like Smit and Green) prefer to think that v. 113 is genuine and that another line, which provided a transition from lust to scheming, has dropped out after v. 112; but this seems less likely.

114-115 *transi*: i.e. say nothing for the moment about their degenerate gymnasia where they wrestle and exercise naked.
       abollae: a thick double cloak. The phrase *magna abolla* seems to have been a colloquial metaphor like our 'big wig'.

116-118 *Stoicus occidit Baream*: Under Nero in A.D. 66 the aristocrat Barea Soranus was prosecuted for treason (Tacitus, *Ann.* 16.30– 32). The Stoic teacher P. Egnatius Celer gave evidence against him, although the accused was both his patron and his pupil.
       senex: this is slightly odd in that there is no evidence for any great disparity in age. J may simply mean that someone of Egnatius' age and occupation should have behaved better.
       ripa: this refers to the river Cydnus which flowed through Tarsus. This was where Egnatius was educated, though he was born in Beirut. So Horace, though born in Venusia, says he was brought up and educated at Rome – *Romae nutriri mihi contigit* (*Epist.* 2.2.41).
       Gorgonei caballi: Pegasus, who sprang from Medusa's blood; the stately periphrasis is undercut by *caballus* 'nag'.
       delapsa est pinna: an incident in the story of Pegasus. J follows the version in which Tarsus received its name from a feather (Gk. *tarsos*) which fell from Pegasus' wing. The more common version connected Tarsus with Pegasus' hoof.

120   The names are meant to evoke a sneer simply by being Greek; but the indefinite *aliquis* and the spondaic ending also help.

121   *gentis vitio*: an unpleasant national characteristic.

122   *solus habet*: (but) keeps him to himself.
       facilem: ready.

123   *exiguum*: a noun.
       naturae: of his own self.

124   *perierunt*: the effect is instantaneous: gone in an instant.

125   *minor*: predicative, 'of less importance'.

126-127 *quod officium . . . quod meritum*: usually attentions and services
         might be expected to win some return. Hence 'what use is a poor
         man's attention and service if . . .?'
         ne nobis blandiar: not to flatter ourselves; i.e. the Romans are
         are also to blame.
         nocte: i.e. before dawn.

129   *vigilantibus orbis*: abl. absolute; *orbis* is feminine, as is shown by
         v. 130. Childless old people were served and flattered by
         captatores who hoped to benefit from their wills. Cf. Pliny, *Epist.*
         2.20; 4.2.2.

130   Albina and Modia are unknown.

131   *servo*: dat.
         cludit latus: the inferior walked on the outside of the superior; cf.
         Horace, *Sat.* 2.5. 17—18. This mark of respect had the practical
         function of protecting the superior from being knocked or
         splashed by the traffic.

132   *alter*: i.e. the slave. A rich man's slave would earn a fair amount in
         tips, but the claim is still wildly exaggerated. The size of a
         tribune's pay is unknown. From this passage one infers it was
         considerable.

133   *Calvinae*: J probably has in mind Junia Calvina, the lively and
         pretty sister of L. Silanus, with whom she was (unjustly) accused
         of incest in A.D. 48 (Tacitus, *Ann.* 12.4 and 8). Here the name is
         used, like Catiena, to typify promiscuous *matronae*.

134   *semel aut iterum*: once or twice.
         palpitet: shudder, i.e. ejaculate.

135-136 *vestiti . . . sella*: these words imply at least a minimal degree of
         elegance. Perhaps the speaker is deliberately avoiding the
         impression that he would have resorted to the lowest type of
         whore. These stood naked in the doorways of their
         establishments.
         dubitas: because of the price.
         Chione: 'Snow-white', the name of a Greek princess (Ovid, *Met.*
         11.301) and of one or more *meretrices* in Martial.

137-138 *da*: produce, here the equivalent of *si dabis*; the apodosis begins
         at *protinus* (140).

hospes numinis Idaei: P. Cornelius Scipio Nasica who, because of his *virtus*, was chosen to carry ashore the image of Cybele brought to Rome from Phrygia in 204 B.C. (Livy, 29.11–14). *Numa*: the most pious of the Roman kings.

138-139 *qui servavit . . . Minervam*: L. Caecilius Metellus rescued the image of Minerva from the blazing temple of Vesta in 241 B.C. The noble effect is undercut by the ridiculous *trepidam*.

140   *ad censum*: sc. some verb like *itur*.

142   *paropside*: dish (Gk.).

144-146 *fidei*: credibility.
iures aras: swear (by) the altars. With *Samothracum* (gen. pl.) and *nostrorum* sc. *deorum*. Samothrace is an island in the N Aegean, where mysteries were celebrated in honour of the Cabiri (for whom see the *Ox. Class. Dict.*). According to the Suda (a 10th cent. Greek encyclopaedia) these divinities punished perjury. A poor man's oath counts for nothing – people think he can lie at will and escape the gods' wrath.

148   *hic idem*: the pauper.

149   *alter calceus*: one shoe.

150-151 Lit. 'or if more than one scar shows the coarse and recent thread where a wound has been sewn together'. Martial 1.103.6 shows that J is referring to a shoe.

154-155 In the Roman theatre the *orchestra* (a semi-circular space in front of the stage) was reserved for senators, and the next fourteen rows for knights.
si pudor est: kindly.
res: the minimum fortune required of a knight was 400,000 sesterces.
legi: the law which established this distinction was the *Lex Roscia Theatralis*, introduced by the tribune L. Roscius Otho in 67 B.C. (see 159.)

156-158 Whoremongers, auctioneers, and gladiators were all despised, and by the *Lex Iulia Municipalis* (44 B.C.) were debarred from office. But they were sometimes quite rich and so their sons might be smartly turned out (*nitidus, cultos*). The *pinnirapus* snatched feathers from the helmet of his heavily-armed opponent; the *lanista* was a manager or trainer.

160   *gener*: predicative, as a son-in-law.

hic: i.e. in Rome.
placuit: ever won acceptance.
censu: modal abl. saying how.
sarcinulis inpar: not up to the girl's dowry (lit. 'little bundles').

161 Since the poor man cannot afford to pamper the *testator* with gifts, he is never made an heir.

162 This may imply that men who were called in by the aediles as consultants were paid handsomely for their services.
agmine facto: in a body.

163 *tenues*: of small substance, hence poor. J is referring to the secessions of the plebs in the early republic.

166 *magno*: abl. of price, sc. *constat*.

167 *frugi*: an indeclinable adjective, here meaning frugal; the form is derived from an original predicative dat.

168-169 *turpe (esse) negabis translatus subito*: if you were suddenly whisked away (by a god).
mensamque Sabellam: or a Samnite table; cf. *Sat.* 10.100 and 170.

170 *veneto duroque cucullo*: a coarse blue hood.

172-174 The order is *si quando ipsa maiestas dierum festorum colitur.* Translate *ipsa* as 'even'.
herboso theatro: performances are so rare that grass grows between the stone seats. There is a good deal of evidence for stone theatres in country towns. See L. Friedlaender, *Sittengeschichte Roms*, ed. Wissowa, vol. 4, 243 – 8. The finest examples are listed by Balsdon, *Life and Leisure* (see bibliography) 334–5.
redit: a contracted perfect; for the tense see GL 567.

175 *exodium*: these 'end-pieces' were short farces on rustic or mythological subjects, performed by type characters wearing masks. They included a good deal of trickery, horseplay, and bawdy humour. See W. Beare, *The Roman Stage*, 3rd ed. (1964) chapters 16 and 17.
pallentis: probably the mask was whitened.

178 *orchestram*: in a country town the occupants of the orchestra would be the municipal senate (*decuriones*).
clari velamen honoris: ' as a robe of high office' in apposition to *tunicae.*

179   *tunicae*: in Rome even the populace (i.e. the free citizen body)
        had to wear the toga in the theatre; in the country a clean white
        tunic was enough.
        summis aedilibus: the chief officials.

180   I.e. we dress more stylishly than we can afford.

181   *sumitur*: i.e. is borrowed.

182   *ambitiosa*: pretentious.

184-185 *Cossum . . . Veiento*: in this context the names are used to typify
        haughty aristocrats; they are associated with the Cornelii Lentuli
        and the Fabricii respectively.

186   *barbam*: sc. *amati.*
        metit . . . deponit: the man is not performing these acts in person.
        A boy's first trim and haircut provided an occasion for a domestic
        celebration.

187-188 The client is expected to pay the slave, take the cake and then
        offer it to the Lares.
        accipe . . . tibi habe: take (the money) and keep your cake. These
        words are probably spoken by the client.

188-189 *praestare tributa (servis)*: the phrase bitterly implies that the
        client is inferior to the slave.
        cultis: smartly dressed.
        peculia: the savings which would buy the slave's freedom.

190-192 *Praeneste*: the modern Palestrina, 23 miles ESE of Rome. Its
        hilly situation made it attractive in hot weather.
        ruinam: the collapse of his house.
        Volsiniis: the modern Bolsena in Etruria, 80 miles NW of Rome.
        Gabiis: between Rome and Praeneste.
        proni Tiburis: the modern Tivoli, on a steep hillside 18 miles ENE
        of Rome.

194   *sic*: i.e. with a weak prop.
        labentibus: masc.; the people are put instead of the house.

196   *pendente ruina*: when the structure is ready to collapse.

198   *poscit aquam*: is shouting 'fire!'

199   *Ucalegon*: taken from *Aen.* 2.311 – 312 – *iam proximus ardet/
        Ucalegon.* This lends an ironical dignity to the poor Roman.
        tibi: dat. of person concerned (GL 350), but no particular person

is addressed.

200   If the alarm is raised at the bottom of the stairs; *ab* indicates the
       source of the action.

201   *tegula*: tile, here in a collective sense.

202   *reddunt*: duly deliver, hence lay. A satirical juxtaposition of harsh
       and gentle.

203   *Cordo*: identified by the scholiast, perhaps wrongly, with the
       poet of 1.2.
       Procula minor: too small for Procula, who was no doubt a female
       dwarf.

204-205 *ornamentum*: in apposition to *urceoli*. The position of the
       cantharus cannot be visualized with confidence; perhaps it stood
       on a shelf beneath the main surface or hung on a hook. The MS
       reading *sub eodem marmore* tells us of the *abacus'* material at a
       point when it no longer seems relevant. According to the con-
       jecture printed here (which is that of Matthias and Housman), a
       marble figure of the centaur Chiron supported the sideboard.

206   *iam* goes with *vetus*; the basket was by now ancient.

207   *opici mures*: Roman mice who couldn't read Greek and had no
       respect for art. See Mayor's note.

208   *enim*: (I assert this) for who denies it?

212   *si*: (but) if.
       Asturici: the name signifies conquests in Spain (where there was
       a district called Asturia) on the analogy of Africanus,
       Macedonicus etc.
       cecidit: as the result of fire, as is shown by v. 214.
       horrida: with hair dishevelled; sc. *est*.

213   *pullati*: dressed in black.
       differt vadimonia: i.e. puts off the day on which a defendant
       must appear. On days of national mourning legal business was
       postponed.

214   *odimus*: we curse.

215   *ardet adhuc*: sc. *Asturici domus*.
       donet: the subjunctive expresses purpose.

216   *inpensas*: building materials.

217-218 *aliquid praeclarum Euphranoris*: Euphranor was a distinguished
sculptor and painter in fourth century Athens. Polyclitus was an
even greater sculptor in the fifth century. See index of G. Richter,
A Handbook of Greek Art, 6th ed. 1969.
aera: Housman's conjecture for the MSS *haec*; these works are
thought of as having once adorned the temples of Asia.

219   *mediam Minervam*: a figure of Minerva, goddess of arts and crafts,
to stand in the middle.

200   *modium argenti*: a bagful of money. Admittedly this is in a
different category from that of the other gifts mentioned, but if
argentum is interpreted as silver plate then a *modius* would not
represent a very significant quantity. Also Mayor's parallels
favour money.
reponit: i.e. in place of what he had.

221-222 Persicus must be the owner of the house, but it is not clear how
his name should be related to Asturicus (212). Perhaps he is
supposed to have lived in a house which was known as the *domus
Asturici* after a former owner; or perhaps both names are meant
to belong to the same man (Groag postulates a historical Fabius
Persicus Asturicus).

223-224 *Sorae . . . Fabrateriae . . . Frusinone*: towns in Latium, not far
from Aquinum.
paratur: can be bought.

225   *tenebras*: a dark hole.

226   *hortulus*: a plot of ground for vegetables.
hic: in the country.
puteus . . . diffunditur: (water from) the well is poured. The well
is so shallow that water can be drawn in a bucket without a rope.

228   *bidentis amans*: wedded to your hoe.

229   *Pythagoreis*: Pythagoreans followed a frugal vegetarian diet.

231   *unius . . . lacertae*: a hyperbolically minute piece of livestock.

232   *vigilando*: through lack of sleep; the *o* is short.

233   *inperfectus*: undigested. Sickness is caused by indigestion, and
indigestion by lack of sleep.

234   *meritoria*: hired lodgings.

235   *magnis opibus*: abl. of price.

236   *raedarum transitus*: vehicles excluded during the day poured in at
       night.

237   *stantis mandrae*: a herd which has been brought to a standstill
       by a traffic jam. It is hard to decide whether the genitive is
       subjective – 'the abuse coming from (the drivers of) the herd' –
       or objective – 'the abuse directed at the herd'.

238   *Druso*: (dat.) the somnolent Claudius, emperor A.D. 41 –54. J
       often treats the dead as existing in a timeless present.
       vitulisque marinis: the elder Pliny says of seals *nullum animal
       graviore somno premitur* (*NH* 9.19).

240   *ingenti . . . Liburna*: apparently metaphorical 'in a huge galley';
       the rich man rides above the waves of humanity; cf. *unda* (244).

242   *clausa . . . fenestra*: if the occupant is to read or write (241)
       this must refer to mica, which admitted light but muffled sound.
       In *Sat.* 1.124–126, however, we have to think of a curtain, as
       profer caput shows.

245   *assere*: the pole of a litter. This whole passage (from 236 to 247
       and also 254 to 256) reappears, transformed, in vv. 99–107 of
       Pope's imitation of Horace, *Epist.* 2.2.

248   *digito*: toe.
       haeret: stamps.

249   *sportula*: here a club picnic, cf. Suetonius, *Claudius* 21. In such
       cases *sportula* sometimes refers to meat as opposed to bread and
       wine.

250   *culina*: lit. 'kitchen'; J is thinking of portable stoves.

251   *Corbulo*: Cn. Domitius Corbulo, the famous general who served
       under Claudius and Nero, was *corpore ingens* (Tacitus, *Ann.*
       13.8).

252   *recto vertice*: with head steady and erect.

254   *longa*: tall, even though it is here horizontal.
       coruscat: sways.

255-256 *serraco*: a heavy goods wagon.
       altera plaustra: 'a second wagon', poetic pl. or 'a second set of
       wagons', though this is not wholly logical.
       nutant: the subject is *abies* and *pinus*.

257   *saxa Ligustica*: marble from Liguria, in particular from Luna near
        the modern Carrara.

260-261 The corpse of every man who is killed (*omne*) is crushed, and
        passes out of existence like the *anima*. Thus the body is
        destroyed, the *anima* (or 'breath of life') is dispersed, and the
        umbra descends to Hades.

262   *unctis*: apparently a conventional epithet; the strigils are 'oily'
        because they have to do with oil.

263   *striglibus*: the syncopated form (for *strigilibus*) is due to metrical
        convenience.
        componit lintea: lays out the towels.
        pleno . . . guto: abl. of attendant circumstances (W 43.5).

265   *ripa*: i.e. by one of the rivers of the underworld.

266   *porthmea*: Gk. acc. for *porthmeus*; Charon.
        nec sperat: and has no hope of (being taken on board).
        alnum: (alder-wood) boat.

267   In effect this explains v. 266.
        trientem: one third of an as, equivalent to the Greek obol; here
        Charon's fare.

269-272 *quod spatium*: sc. *sit*. *quod spatium*, *quotiens* and *quanto
        pondere* are all indirect questions after *respice*; since, in these
        clauses, (b) and (c) refer to potsherds, (a) probably does so too;
        hence *testa* probably means a potsherd rather than a tile, and
        tectis buildings rather than roofs.
        silicem: pavement.
        ignavus: negligent.

273   *casus*: objective gen. This word for misadventure is appropriate in
        a context full of falling objects.

274-275 *adeo*: so true is it that; hence 'for'. 'There are as many forms of
        death as there are windows watching with open shutters on that
        night as you pass by.'

276   *optes . . . feras*: jussive subjunctives (W 109 and 126 n.2).

277   *contentae*: sc. *fenestrae*. For the personification cf. *vigiles* (275).
        pelves: i.e. their contents.

278   *petulans*: aggressive.
        forte: for some reason.

279-280 *noctem . . . Pelidae*: a night like that suffered by Peleus' son. In
Iliad 24.10 Achilles, the son of Peleus, cannot sleep for grief and
remorse at the death of his friend Patroclus.
Pelidae: gen. sing. of *Pelides*. For declension of Gk. substantives
see GL 65.

281   *ergo* is wrong in sense (we would expect *nam*) and metrically
dubious (J does not elsewhere have a long o when the ictus falls
on the first syllable); *quibusdam* blurs the central position of the
youth who is *ebrius* (278) and *mero fervens* (283); and the whole
line spoils the rhetorical effect. It probably arose from a marginal
note (*non aliter poterit dormire*) explaining v. 282. See
Housman's ed. xxxv and xliii.

282   *improbus annis*: 'young hothead' (Green); *improbus* implies a
a disregard of civilised rules;
annis: abl. of cause (GL 408).

283   *coccina laena*: the colour (scarlet) was expensive, the material
(fleece) was thick and warm.

285   Lit. 'a quantity of flames, moreover, and a bronze lamp', hence
'the flames from numerous bronze lamps'. Again the material
implies affluence. There was no street-lighting in Rome.

290   *stari*: an impersonal passive. Lit. 'he orders a halt to be made'.

291   *quid agas*: the second person now refers to the victim (contrast
v. 289); the subjunctive is deliberative.

292   *aceto*: cheap sour wine.

293   *conche*: *conchis* (fem.) was a kind of bean.
tumes: implies flatulence.
sectile porrum: leeks were often cut above the ground as the
leaves shot up and eaten like chives.

294   *elixi vervecis labra*: i.e. a boiled sheep's head.
comedit: has been scoffing

295   *calcem*: as the toes were unprotected the heel was used for
kicking.

296   *ubi consistas*: where you have your stand (as a beggar).
quaero: the indicative has a deliberative sense (W 172 n).

298-299 *vadimonia faciunt*: they take you to court.

301   *paucis*: (at least) a few.

302   *metuas*: see n. on 276, though the construction is more common
        in prohibitions as here.
        spoliet: a subjunctive of purpose.

303-304 *clausis domibus*: abl. absolute.
        postquam ɛ ̣ic.: lit. 'when every shutter everywhere belonging to a
        chained shop has been secured and has fallen silent.'

307   The Pomptine marshes covered an area of 28 x 8 miles on either
        side of the Via Appia as it ran NW from Anxur. The Gallinarian
        pine-forest was in the west of Campania between the Vulturnus
        and Cumae.

308   *sic . . . tamquam ad vivaria*: as if to preserves (where game or fish
        was fattened for the table).

309   I.e. *qua fornace, qua incude non graves catenae (sunt)?*

310   *maximus modus*: the greatest amount of iron goes into fetters.

312   The sequence was *pater, avus, proavus, abavus, atavus, tritavus.*

313   *tribunis*: not the *tribuni plebis* but the *tribuni militares consulari
        potestate* who were occasionally appointed in the early republic
        and were the highest officials in the state.

314   *carcere*: the *carcer Mamertinus*; cf. Livy 1.33.8.

315   *alias . . . et pluris*: many other.
        poteram: I could; cf. Virgil, *Ecl.* 1.79.

317-318 *iamdudum adnuit*: has long been signalling; the verb is present
        tense (GL 230).
        vale nostri memor: goodbye and don't forget me.

319   *tuo Aquino*: this is the main evidence that Aquinum was J's home
        town.

320   *Helvinam*: presumably the temple was built by a Helvius; for this
        gens in these parts see *CIL* 10, index p. 1039.
        vestramque: probably 'of your townsmen', but 'of your family' is
        also possible.

321   *ni pudet illas*: if the *saturae* are not embarrassed by Umbricius'
        heavy boots (*caligatus*). A smiling conclusion.

QUESTIONS FOR DISCUSSION

1.   Is Umbricius the mouth-piece of Juvenal himself? If you think not, can you say where the two differ?

2.   If Umbricius' views *are* those of Juvenal, does Juvenal emerge as an admirable character? If you think he doesn't, is this merely the subjective view of a twentieth century reader? And was Juvenal *aware* of being unpleasant?

3.   Does Juvenal make a clear distinction between attractive country and dreadful city? Or between virtuous antiquity and the vicious present?

4.   Is the satire sufficiently similar to Virgil's first Eclogue to justify a comparison?

SUGGESTED EXERCISES

1.   Notice how the motif of escape recurs through the poem, cutting across the divisions of subject-matter.

2.   Examine Juvenal's use of Greek names and words and his references to Greek mythology, literature, art, and philosophy. Is the attitude which emerges a simple one?

3.   Read the satire along with Johnson's *London*.

FURTHER READING

G. W. Bowersock, *Augustus and the Greek World*, Oxford 1965.

M. D. George, *London Life in the Eighteenth Century*, London 1930.

N. Rudd, *Johnson's Juvenal*, Bristol Classical Press 1981.

A. N. Sherwin-White, *Racial Prejudice in Imperial Rome*, Cambridge 1967.

Z. Yavetz, 'The Living Conditions of the Roman Plebs', *The Crisis of the Roman Republic*, ed. R. Seager, Heffer 1969.

SATIRE X

THEME: most prayers are misguided and, if answered, harmful.

STRUCTURE: 1—53 introduction: men's aspirations and the attitude of
Democritus; 54—114 political power; 114—132 eloquence;
133—187 military glory; 188—288 long life; 289—345 beauty;
346—366 conclusion: harmless prayers.

IDEAS: cf. [Plato] *Alcibiades* 2; Valerius Maximus (a writer of the first
cent. A.D. who made a collection of historical *exempla*) 7.2
Ext. 1.; and, with reference to Democritus and the *tranquilla vita*
of v. 364, Seneca, *De tranquillitate animi*; Plutarch *Peri
Euthymias* ('On Cheerfulness') in the *Moralia* (Loeb Classical
Library Vol. 6). Several of Juvenal's *exempla* occur in the
Declamationes attributed to Quintilian and in the *Suasoriae* of
the elder Seneca.

1   *Gadibus*: Cadiz, representing the extreme West.
        usque: preposition.

3   *illis*: dat.
        multum diversa: 'greatly different'.

4   *ratione*: adverbial abl.

5   *dextro pede*: to set out with the right foot was a good omen;
        hence 'auspiciously'. Cf. Petronius, *Satyricon* 30.

6   *conatūs*: gen. after *paeniteat*.

7   *evertēre*: *everterunt*.
        domus: households.

8   *faciles*: obliging.
        togā: in peace time.

10-11   For example Milo of Croton, a famous strongman who lived
        c. 500 B.C., tried to rend with his bare hands an oak which had
        been half split by wedges. The wedges fell out, the tree trapped
        his hands, and he was killed by wolves.

viribus: with both *confisus* and *periit*.
periīt: the vowel in the final syllable preserves its original quantity.

12   *pluris*: acc.

13   *strangulat*: smothers.
      cuncta: 'all other'.

14   *ballaena Britannica*: Drusus (from 12 B.C.) and Germanicus (from A.D. 14) had opened the North Sea to the Romans, and the victories of Suetonius Paulinus (from A.D. 59) and Iulius Agricola (from A.D. 77) had drawn attention to Britain. The whale is thought of as a monster.

15   Nero's reign of terror began after the death of Burrus in A.D. 62.

16   *Longinum*: i.e. his house. Following Piso's conspiracy (A.D. 65) C. Cassius Longinus, an eminent jurist and a former governor of Syria, was banished to Sardinia. See Tacitus, *Ann.* 16.7 and 9.
      Senecae: Seneca the Younger, b. in Corduba in S Spain about 2 B.C., was tutor and later adviser to Nero. His enormous wealth did not prevent him from writing numerous essays and epistles on Stoic ethics. In A.D. 65 he was forced to commit suicide for allegedly participating in the conspiracy of Piso.

17   *Lateranorum*: Plautius Lateranus, consul designate in A.D. 65, was implicated in Piso's conspiracy and put to death (Tacitus, *Ann.* 15.60). His house was confiscated.
      obsidet: historic present.

18   *cenacula*: poetic plural.

19   *puri*: plain, not embossed.

20   *contum*: 'pike', or possibly 'boat-hook' if J is thinking of the Pomptine marshes (cf. *harundinis* in v. 21).

22   *cantabit*: translate literally. What J has in mind is blithe indifference; as so often, he exaggerates for rhetorical effect.

24   *divitiae*: predicate; *sunt* is understood.

25   *arca*: bankers kept their clients' *arcae* in the temple of Castor in the forum.
      aconita: a poison derived from a plant.

26   *illa*: i.e. *aconita*.

27   *Setinum*: the wine of Setia, an ancient town in Latium, was in many people's opinion superior even to Falernian. *ardebit* refers to the wine's colour.

28   *iamne*: i.e. after what I've just said. The *-ne* here has the same force as *nonne* (GL 454 n.5). The two philosophers are Democritus and Heraclitus.

        Democritus of Abdera (5th and early 4th century B.C.) was known in later antiquity as 'the laughing philosopher' because of his treatise 'On Cheerfulness'. A man of powerful and wide-ranging intellect, he was one of the pioneers of the atomic theory, which was taken over by Epicurus.

        Heraclitus of Ephesus, writing c. 500 B.C., maintained that the universe was a ceaseless conflict of opposites regulated by law. His fragments give the impression of an austere, oracular personality, and according to Theophrastus he suffered from 'melancholia' (Diogenes Laertius 9.6). The contrast between him and Democritus, which was apparently introduced by Seneca's teacher Sotion, was popularized by Seneca himself; see *De tranquillitate animi* 15.2 and *De ira* 2.10.5.

29   *ridebat quotiens . . . moverat*: for the iterative construction see GL 567.

30   *auctor*: authority.

31   *rigidi*: harsh.

32   That is, where did he (Heraclitus) get enough moisture for his eyes? *ille humor* is the *humor* implied in *flebat* (30).

34   *essent*: J never uses the indicative with *quamquam*.
       illis: of those days.

35   *praetextae*: a toga with a purple border was worn by consuls, praetors, and curule aediles.
       trabeae: a short purple toga with a scarlet border was worn by equites on ceremonial occasions.
       fasces: bundles of rods with an axe in the middle were carried by lictors as a symbol of the magistrate's power.
       lectica: litters were used by the wealthy and fashionable.
       tribunal: a platform on which curule chairs were set.

36-46   The *pompa Circensis*, which preceded the races, marched from the Capitol through the forum to the Circus. The presiding magistrate rode in a chariot wearing the dress of a triumphant

general.
curribus: poetic plural.

37   *sublimem pulvere*: lit. 'elevated in the dust', i.e. 'high above the dust'.

38   The tunic embroidered with palms and the gold-embroidered purple toga were borrowed for the occasion from the treasury of Jupiter Capitolinus.
        pictae Sarrana etc.: lit. 'wearing from his shoulders the Tyrian hangings of the embroidered toga'. Sarra was an old name for Tyre. *aulaea* emphasizes the absurd size of the garment.

39-40   'So great a circle of a huge crown.'

41   *publicus* and *servus* go together; there is just one slave in the chariot.
        consul: in view of *praetorem* (36), which refers to the same scene, the change of title is hard to justify. The praetor was the magistrate who performed this function; see Mayor on 8.194. E.C. suggests that *consul* may be an inaccurate gloss on an original *praeses*.
        sibi ne placeat: success might lead to presumption and so attract the wrath of Nemesis.

43   *da*: *adde*.
        volucrem: an eagle.
        surgit: surmounts.

44-45   'The long train of dutiful clients walking in front.'
        officia: abstract for concrete.

46   *defossa*: stowed away.
        quos: the antecedent is *Quirites*.

47   *ad*: 'at' going with *invenit*, the subject of which is Democritus.

50   *vervecum*: sheep represented stupidity.
        crasso sub aere: in a thick climate. Democritus' home town (*patria*) was Abdera on the S coast of Thrace. Its citizens were supposed to be dull-witted. Juvenal probably knew nothing about Abdera; he is simply repeating the widely held view that climate affects intelligence.

52-53   'He would tell Fortune to go and hang herself.' In the gesture described the projecting middle finger originally represented the male organ, as the v-sign originally represented the female.
        cum: while (GL 585r. and W 235).

54-55   *quae*: with both *supervacua* and *perniciosa*. 'To cover the knees of the gods with wax' — i.e. with wax tablets containing *vota*. As wax was used to fasten the tablets onto the knees, this idea may also be included.

57   *mergit* is co-ordinate with *praecipitat* (56); there is no conjunction.

58   *pagina*: 'column' or 'list' of honours on the bases of statues.

59   *inpacta* from *inpingo* 'I drive' or 'smash'; the direct object is usually a fist or (as here) a weapon.

60   Animals which were unruly sometimes had their legs broken. *caballus* here implies a satirical mixture of pity and condescension: 'poor old nags'.

61   Bellows and furnace bring a glow to the head.

62   *adoratum*: Tiberius allowed images of Sejanus to be worshipped. *populo*: dat. (GL 354).

63   *Seianus*: L. Aelius Sejanus acquired immense power as prefect of the praetorian guard under Tiberius. This power increased when Tiberius retired to Capri in A.D. 27. In A.D. 31 Sejanus was apparently forming a plot to assassinate Tiberius, but the emperor was warned in good time and sent a letter to the senate. As a result Sejanus was arrested and executed. (See the index to Syme's *Tacitus* under Aelius Sejanus.) In his tragedy *Sejanus his fall* Ben Jonson draws extensively on the scene described by Juvenal.

64   Pitchers, basins, saucepans, and chamber pots.

65   'The outer door of a house was decorated with laurel on occasions of public or private rejoicing' (Duff).

66   *cretatum*: dark spots would be covered with pipe clay to ensure ritual purity.
ducitur unco: corpses of criminals were dragged by a hook, which passed around the jaw, from the prison to the *scalae Gemoniae*, where they were left for three days; they were then thrown into the river.

67-68   *quis . . . vultus*: the combination *quis puer* is at least as common as *qui puer*.

68-69   The speaker is to be imagined as a former acquaintance of Sejanus.

70   An *index* betrays his accomplices; a *delator* brings a charge from outside.

71   For the letter see Dio Cassius 58.9–10.

72   Tiberius had been on Capri since A.D. 27.
        bene habet: 'right'.

73   *turba Remi*: the plebs. *Rōmuli* does not fit a hexameter. *sequitur Fortunam* is explained by what follows.

74   *Nortia*: the Etruscan goddess of Fortune. She was worshipped at Volsinii, the birthplace of Sejanus (*Tusco*).

75-76   'If the elderly princeps had been caught off guard and struck down.'
        senectus principis: this form of expression is used for variety and metrical convenience. Sometimes it emphasizes the attribute of the person concerned (here age) or lends an aura of grandeur, but such effects are not always obvious.

77-78   *iam pridem* is here used with the perfect because the action of *effudit* is over, whereas in *ex quo . . . vendimus* the present tense indicates that the action is still going on (GL 230). Trans. 'since we stopped selling our votes to anyone'. The use of *vendimus* instead of the expected *damus* adds a sardonic allusion to the bribery which had marked the last century of the republic. Since A.D. 14 magistrates had been elected by the senate, not by the popular assemblies.

77   *Augustum*: the first emperor's cognomen was adopted by his successors.

79-80   *se continet*: 'restrains itself,' a sarcastic phrase.

81   *circenses*: sc. *ludi*.
        perituros: for the fortunes of Sejanus' associates see Mayor's notes.

82   *magna est fornacula*: i.e. 'many will find it hot' (Duff).
        pallidulus: there may possibly be a play on Bruttidius' cognomen (see next note); so Ferguson.

83   *Bruttidius*: Bruttidius Niger, an accomplished orator; aedile in A.D. 22. According to Tacitus *Ann*. 3.66 he was a man of impatient ambition. The Altar of Mars was on the Campus Martius.

84-85   'I fear our defeated Ajax (i.e. Tiberius) may take vengeance for being badly defended.' Ajax, defeated by Ulysses in the contest for Achilles' arms, resolved to murder Agamemnon, Menelaus, and Ulysses. He was made mad by Athena and slew a flock of sheep instead. The comparison is unsatisfactory, since *victus* does not suit Tiberius and *male defensus* does not apply to Ajax. Yet the idea of mad revenge on innocent victims remains, and other interpretations are weaker still.

87-88   A slave could testify against his master on a charge of treason. *cervice obstricta*: 'with a noose around his neck'.

90   *salutari*: to be waited on respectfully at the morning *salutatio*.

91-92   *illi . . . illum*: one man . . . another.
        curules: sc. *sellas*; in view of *summas* this is probably a poetic plural = 'the consulship'.

93-94   Tiberius sits on the rock of goats (*Capreae*) with his herd (*grex*) of Chaldean astrologers. J is thinking especially of Thrasyllus, whom Tiberius had brought with him from Rhodes.

95   *egregios equites*: knights whose fathers had been free born and who possessed the senatorial census of 1,000,000 sesterces were selected by the emperor to become *procuratores Augusti*. In their preliminary period of military service many such men might have been tribunes in the praetorian guard under Sejanus.
        castra domestica: 'a barrack as part of your household.' Sejanus brought the praetorians together into a fixed base; cf. Tacitus, *Ann.* 4.2.

95-96   'Why *shouldn't* you desire these things?' The subjunctive is deliberative (W 173).

97   *tanti (sunt) ut* etc.: 'are worth such a price that the amount of evil they entail equals the joy they bring.'

99   *huius*: Sejanus. He was given the *ornamenta praetoria* in A.D. 20 and so had the right to wear the *toga praetexta* of curule magistrates.

100   Fidenae, Gabii, and Ulubrae were Latin towns which had dwindled in size and importance.
        potestas: abstract for concrete; cf. 'the powers that be.'

101   Local aediles would try people who had given short measure. *pannosus* is a piece of metropolitan condescension.

106-107 *tabulata*: storeys.

'Thus ensuring that the fall would be all the greater and that once the structure had been pushed over its collapse would be devastating.' In the *unde* clause the disastrous result is represented ironically as intended. *praeceps* is a noun.

108   *Crassos . . . Pompeios*: men like Crassus and Pompey.

Marcus Licinius Crassus made a fortune from the Sullan proscriptions. Later, after defeating Spartacus, he was consul with Pompey in 70 B.C. He played a major part in the political intrigues of the 60s and eventually, in 55, obtained a military command in Syria. Two years later he was killed at Carrhae.

Gnaeus Pompeius Magnus was granted unprecedented powers to deal with the pirates (67 B.C.) and Mithridates (66 B.C.). When he returned from the east in 62 he was at the height of his career. Although he joined the first triumvirate with Caesar and Crassus in 60 and renewed it in 56 his relations with Caesar steadily deteriorated until the latter crossed the Rubicon in 49. After his defeat at Pharsalus in 48 Pompey fled to Egypt but was assassinated on his arrival.

illum: Julius Caesar. J is thinking here of his dictatorship. The phrasing is appropriate to the control of slaves or animals.

111   *magna vota*: prayers for greatness.

112   *generum Cereris*: Pluto, king of the world below.

113   *sicca mors*: the opposite of 'a sticky death'.

115   *quinquatribus*: from *quinquatrūs*, a festival of Minerva, goddess of arts and crafts, lasting from March 19–23. For *totus* and the abl. expressing duration cf. v. 206 and see W 54 n.1.

116   *adhuc*: 'as yet', with *uno*. The *as* was paid into Minerva's treasury.
       parcam: this seems to imply that Minerva is sparing with her gifts – i.e. not many achieve eminence in her arts. Cf. *Parca non mendax* in Horace, *Odes* 2.16.39.

118   *perīt*: a contracted perfect.

119   *leto dedit*: a very old formula, but one cannot be sure that it carries an ironical nuance here since Ovid (*Met*. 1.670) uses it in a neutral way.

120   *ingenio*: probably abl. of cause, like *eloquio* in v. 118. Some take it as a dat. ('genius had its hand and head cut off'), but this seems

rather less likely in that Demosthenes' *ingenium* has also just been mentioned (v. 119). On Antony's instructions Cicero's head and hands were cut off and displayed on the *rostra* in the forum (43 B.C.).
nec umquam: = *sed numquam*; cf. Catullus 22.15.

122   Cicero as consul suppressed the conspiracy of Catiline in 63 B.C. He subsequently wrote an epic poem *De consulatu suo*. In the line quoted, thought and sound produce an effect which Cicero did not intend. One recalls Horace's dictum: *professus grandia turget* (*Ars Poetica* 27).
     Romam: accusative of exclamation.

123   An allusion to Cicero, *Phil.* 2.118: *contempsi Catilinae gladios, non pertimescam tuos* (i.e. Antony's). Juvenal means that if all Cicero's writings had been so feeble he would not have antagonized Antony. As it was, the fourteen *Philippics* (so called after Demosthenes' speeches against Philip) proved fatal.

124   *malo*: they are preferable because safer.

125   *Philippica*: vocative.
     famae: genitive of quality (GL 365).

126   'who are unrolled next after first', i.e. the second Philippic.
     illum: Demosthenes, who had inspired the Athenians to resist Philip, was condemned to death and poisoned himself in 322 B.C.

128   River and charioteer are metaphors for the grand style.
     theatri: the people's assembly sometimes met in the theatre of Dionysus.

129   Demosthenes' end indicated that the gods were hostile to him from the start.

130-132   Demosthenes' father was a gentleman who derived part of his income from a sword factory. Juvenal's blacksmith is a squalid caricature.

132   *Vulcano*: Vulcan is used by metonymy for Vulcan's work.

133-136   In apposition to *exuviae* we have *lōrīca, buccula, iugum, aplustre* and *captivŏs* (which is nom. case — see GL 31). *truncis tropaeis* is a poetic plural, lit. 'trophies with branches chopped off', the 'trophy' being originally a tree with the remains of a few branches on which the spoils were fastened. A possible translation would be 'a breastplate fastened to a mutilated tree of victory'.
     tēmōne: ablative of separation (GL 390).

aplustre: a wooden ornament projecting above the stern. It might
have the shape of a bird's wing or a fish's tail, and it held a staff
hung with coloured ribbons.
arcu: a triumphal arch.

137   *humanis maiora bonis*: 'greater than human (i.e. divine) blessings'.
137-139 *se . . . erexit*: 'aspired'.
       induperator: *Impĕrātor* does not fit the hexameter; also the
       archaic form has a grander sound which enhances the satirical
       effect.

139-140 Lit. 'from there he had reasons', i.e. these rewards provided the
       reason for enduring peril and toil.
       tanto: ablative of measure of difference (GL 403).

141   *ipsam*: for her own sake.
       tollas: one removes (W 119).

142   *olim*: before now.

143   *gloria*: not 'glory' but 'the passion for glory'.
       tituli: an inscription recording the general's exploits.

144-146 *ad quae*: This adds the satirist's comment: even tombs decay.
       And the desire for posthumous renown is frustrated by a plant
       which lives for only one generation.
       mala robora: 'rude strength' (Ramsay).

147   *Hannibalem*: i.e. his ashes.

148-150 *non capit*: 'cannot contain'. Africa is 'pounded by the Moorish
       ocean (i.e. the Atlantic)' and reaches 'to the warm Nile as far
       south as Ethiopia'; *rursus* here means 'backwards' (i.e. 'south-
       wards') — an archaic sense.
       aliosque elephantos: 'the other kind of elephant', i.e. other than
       the Indian, which J refers to in 11.125 (preferred by E.C.).
       Or J may mean 'the other area of elephants'; one area was in
       Mauretania (cf. *Mauro oceano* in 148f.), another was in Ethiopia.
       See *Sat.* 11.124f. and Pliny the Elder, *NH* 8.32. (preferred by
       N.R.). Here, as in Statius, *Theb.* 10.85 and Valerius Flaccus, *Arg.*
       2.382, the first of the two items in question is not mentioned and
       has to be mentally supplied with the second.

151-153 In 221 B.C. Hannibal took over command of the Carthaginian
       army in Spain. He crossed the Pyrenees in 218 and the Alps later
       in the same year. Note the massive *Pȳrēnaeūm* and the choice of
       transilit. The idea of hybris comes out even more strongly in
       vv. 152–153. On the use of vinegar Appian says 'He burned wood

and threw water and vinegar on the burning ashes. After making the rock brittle in this way he smashed it with sledgehammers' (*Bell. Hann.* 4). cf. Livy 21.37.

154   *iam*: after Cannae in 216 B.C.

154   'He persists in pressing on.'

155   *acti*: partitive gen. (GL 369).
        Poeno milite: abl. of instrument.

156   *Subura*: We might have expected the Capitol; instead we get the Subura, a seedy district between the Viminal and the Esquiline.

157   *qualis facies*: 'What a sight!'

158   *Gaetula*: from what is now Morocco and Algeria.
        luscum: Hannibal lost the sight of one eye through infection when crossing the marshes of the Arno in 217 B.C. (Livy 22.2.10–11).

159   *vincitur*: Hannibal was defeated by Scipio at Zama (100 miles SW of Carthage) in 202 B.C.

160-162 *nempe*: if you please.
        in exilium: Hannibal left Carthage in 195 B.C. for fear of being handed over to the Romans. He went first to Antiochus of Syria and eventually to Prusias of Bithynia. Juvenal represents him as a humble client at the palace waiting for the king to get up. In 183 or 182 Hannibal took poison, which he carried in a ring, to avoid extradition to the Romans.

163   *miscuit*: 'turned upside down.'

164   *dabunt*: the future, announcing destiny: 'will put'.

166   *anulus*: Note the slight pause after v. 165, the dactylic word filling the first foot, and then the full stop. After Cannae Hannibal had sent home to Carthage quantities of gold rings taken from the Roman dead: hence *vindex* and *ultor*.

166-167 Hannibal's gigantic achievements are summed up and dismissed with these jeering words. Again result is ironically presented as intention (cf. 106–107).
        declamatio: see 1.16 n.

168   *Pellaeo iuveni*: Alexander was born at Pella in Macedonia, which by J's time was a rather insignificant town; he died at Babylon

in 323 B.C. in his 33rd year. When told that there were many
worlds he cried *me miserum quod ne uno quidem adhuc sum
potitus* (Valerius Maximus 8.14. *Ext.* 2).

169   *infelix*: ironical; 'poor fellow'.
          limite: abl. of cause.

170   *ut clausus*: *ut si clausus esset*. Gyara and Seriphus were two of
          the Cyclades, used for political prisoners; cf. 1.73.

171   *urbem*: Babylon. 'The city fortified by potters' (i.e. with bricks)
          is a satirical periphrasis.

173-174 *olim* with *velificatus*. The phrase *velificatus Athos* is meant to
          sound absurd, but Herodotus' account of Xerxes' canal through
          the peninsula of Mt. Athos (7.22−23) is confirmed by
          archaeologists.
          quidquid etc.: 'whatever else lying Greece has the effrontery
          to say (about that campaign) in its history books.'

175-176 *constratum . . . mare*: the sea covered with ships − a sight which
          pleased Xerxes as he sat on his marble throne on the hillside
          (Herodotus 7.45).
          suppositumque rotis: this refers to the bridge over the Hellespont
          (Herodotus 7.36). Housman punctuated *historia; . . . mare
          credimus*, etc.

177-178 *defecisse amnes* is explained by *epotaque flumina*. Cf. Herodotus
          7.21.
          Sostratus: an unidentified poet (*cantat*).
          madidis . . . alis: the poet's gesticulations make his armpits sweat.
          In 5.101 Auster dries his damp wings in Aeolus' prison-house
          (*siccat madidas in carcere pinnas*) − a place which was in J's
          mind (181 below); cf. Ovid, *Met.* 1.264. In view of these refer-
          ences to wings a possible secondary meaning might be that
          Sostratus' inspiration does not take him far off the ground; cf.
          Ovid, *Ars* 1.233-234.

179   *Salamine*: Xerxes' fleet was defeated in 480 B.C. off the island
          of Salamis.

180   *Corus*: the WNW wind;
          Eurus: the ESE. J implies that the storm was caused by the clash
          of opposing winds.
          solitus: J generalizes from one (alleged) case. See Herodotus 7.35,
          where Xerxes is said to have ordered 300 lashes to be inflicted on
          the sea.

181   *Aeolio ... carcere*: Aeolus was put in charge of the winds by his father Jupiter (*Odyssey* 10.21). He kept them imprisoned in a cave (*Aen.* 1.52).

182   *Ennosigaeum*: 'Earthshaker' — a Homeric term for Poseidon/ Neptune. The ancients believed that earthquakes were caused by water forcing its way into subterranean hollows.

183   'That, indeed, was relatively mild. Why he even believed he deserved a branding! What god would have chosen (W 121) to serve such a master?' Herodotus (7.35) records the rumour that Xerxes had the sea branded; Plutarch (*De cohib. ira* 5.455d) states it as a fact. It seems rather unlikely that J would have denied this crowning absurdity. Moreover, the usual text (viz. *quod ... credidit* taking up the *id*) does not provide so direct a lead-in to the question *huic ... deorum*. So the balance of probabilities seems to favour E. W. Weber's conjecture, which we have printed.
     servire: Neptune had served Laomedon, and Apollo Admetus.

185   The suggestion that Xerxes returned straight from Salamis and in a single ship is historically inaccurate but rhetorically effective.

186   *per densa cadavera*: this explains *tarda* as well as providing a description.

187   A concluding statement. *totiens* goes with *exegit*.

189   *recto voltu*: this difficult expression may mean 'when your colour is normal' (i.e. when you are in good health) as opposed to *pallidus*. In v. 300 below *voltum sanguine ferventem* is used of a blushing face; in 6.401 *recta facie* means, according to the scholiast, 'with an unblushing countenance'. Others prefer to take *recto voltu* as referring to the self-assurance which comes from a clear conscience as opposed to the pallor of apprehension.

191   *ante omnia*: first and foremost.

194   *pandit*: spreads.
     Thabraca: on the coast of N Africa S of Sardinia. J is talking of the Barbary apes. The dignity of this line, which may have been taken from another poet, is destroyed in v. 195.

195   *iam*: word order and rhythm would suggest that *iam* went with *mater*: 'a female ape, now a mother'. But this would imply that the female ape did not bear young until late in life, which is not only false but also so odd an idea that J can hardly have believed it to be generally accepted. Perhaps, then, *iam* should be taken as

'long since' − a sense which would be aided by the preceding *vetula*. This seems less unlikely than taking *vetula iam bucca* together. For *iam mater* Ferguson ingeniously conjectures *Garamantis* (African), comparing *Aen*. 4.198.

197   We have printed without much confidence Housman's emend-ation of the unmetrical *hoc atque alio* found in the best manuscript (P). Other MSS read *hoc atque ille alio*. For Housman's arguments see p.liii of his second edition. He gives the sense as 'one is handsomer than another and differently featured (*ore alio*), this is sturdier far than that: the old are all alike.' Any conjecture must convey the idea of appearance.

198   The features mentioned illustrate the statement *una senum facies*.

200   *misero*: dat. of agent; 'the poor creature'.
       gingiva . . . inermi: gums which have lost their cutting edge.

201-202 The expression is illogical but the meaning is clear enough, i.e. he is so revolting that he disgusts not only his own family but even a legacy-hunter. Cossus is unknown.

203   *torpente palato*: as the palate loses its sensitivity.

204   '(I don't count impotence) for . . .'

205   *coneris*: the subject is indefinite; hence the subjunctive.
       ramice: with a varicocele, i.e. an enlargement of the veins of the spermatic cord or those of the scrotum.

208   *suspecta*: the suspicion is that he calls for oral stimulation.

209   *partis*: faculty.

210-212 *cantare* can be used (a) of one who sings, (b) of one who accom-panies himself on the harp, and (c) of one who plays the pipe. (a) is represented by *cantante*, (b) by (*cantante*) *citharoedo Seleuco*, and probably both (b) and (c) by (*cantantibus eis*) *quibus mos est fulgere*. Gorgeous costumes were worn in the theatre by both harpists and pipers. 'For what pleasure does he have whether in a singer (however outstanding) or in the harpist Seleucus and the others who regularly glitter in their golden mantles?'

213   *quid refert*: 'what does it matter?', followed by an indirect question construction.

216   *puer*: the slave who answered the door. Slaves were sent out to

get the time from public water-clocks and sun-dials. To ask the time was *horas quaerere*, to tell it was *horas nuntiare*.

220   *expediam*: probably pres. subjunctive rather than fut. indicative in view of *promptius*.
amaverit: one might expect this to mean 'has had intercourse with' rather than 'has been in love with', yet it is not easy to find an example of the former use with a feminine subject, and the second allows a more effective climax in vv. 223–224.

220-224 The figures named cannot be identified. Themison recalls the famous doctor mentioned by Seneca (*Epist.* 95.9) and Celsus (3.4), but he could be a more recent and familiar character. A homosexual Hamillus is mentioned in Martial 7.62, but again if J has a real person in mind he could be a ccntemporary (*inclinet* being pres. tense). We may, however, be dealing with types rather than individuals.
autumno: according to the medical writer Celsus (2.1) autumn was the most dangerous season because of its changeable weather. It was the worst season for malaria (Celsus 2.8.42).
socios: business partners.

226   Repeated from 1.25. *mihi*: dat. of personal interest (GL 350).

231   *tantum*: that is all he can manage to do.

232   *ieiuna*: a detail retained from *Iliad* 9.323, which J is echoing. *omni*: any.

233   *maior* is attracted to the gender of *dementia*; strictly it should be neuter agreeing with *damnum* understood.

237   He forbids his own kith and kin to be heirs.

238-239 'So much power has the breath of that artful mouth which stood for sale for many years in the cell of a brothel.' Phiale's sweet breath turns the old man to a jelly. The *fornix* where she once worked would have been under an archway; the pluperfect *steterat* indicates that she is now retired. The phrasing of v. 239 suggests *fellatio*.

240   *ut vigeant*: concessive (GL 608).

242   *plenaeque sororibus urnae*: this should be translated literally; to mention ashes ruins the effect.

246   *rex Pylius*: Nestor, who lived through three generations of men (*Iliad* 1.250; *Odyssey* 3.245).

247   *vitae*: longevity.
        a cornice secundae: 'second (counting) from the crow;' i.e.
        second only to the crow — a bird whose long life was proverbial.

248   *nimirum*: ironical.

249   The indicative is not uncommon in *qui* clauses of reason.
        iam dextra conputat: the ancients counted units and tens on the
        left hand, hundreds and thousands on the right.

252   *stamine*: thread of life.
        acris: spirited in battle.

253   *Antilochi*: Nestor's son.
        ardentem: i.e. on the pyre.

256   *Peleus*: father of Achilles. Supply *queritur* from *queratur* (251).

257   *alius*: Laertes, father of Ulysses.
        fas: natural.
        Ithacum . . . natantem: 'the swimming Ithacan', with particular
        reference to Ulysses' swim to the coast of Phaeacia (*Odyssey*
        5.374–453). Apparently *nato* with a personal subject was not
        used in the sense of 'I sail'.

258-264 *incolumi Troia*: abl. absolute.
        venisset: apodosis; the protasis is in v. 263; for the terms see
        GL 589.
        Assaracus: son of Tros and brother of Priam's grandfather Ilus.
        sollemnibus: abl. of manner (GL 399) from the noun *sollemne*.
        funus: corpse.
        Hectore . . . cervicibus: 'Hector and the other brothers . . . on
        their shoulders.' For 'neck' = our 'shoulder' cf. 1.64.
        ut: take with *primos*, 'as soon as'. Cassandra and Polyxena,
        Priam's daughters, are said to begin the ritual lamentation.
        inciperet takes its mood from the conditional form of the whole
        sentence. *audaces* of misguided daring. With the reference to
        Paris' ships cf. *Iliad* 5.62–64.

267-270 *miles*: in apposition to Priam who is the subject of *tulit*.
        tiara: the Phrvgian head-gear, a kind of fez.
        bos: for the monosyllabic thud cf. *procumbit humi bos* (*Aen.*
        5.481).
        ingrato: the ploughman's attitude is ascribed to the plough. For
        Priam's death cf. *Aen.* 2.506–558.

271-275 *utcumque*: at any rate.
        torva: not attributive with *uxor* but part of the predicate with

latravit.

vixerat: an aorist (GL 241 n.1). The *uxor* was Hecuba.

273-275 *regem Ponti*: Mithridates (120–63 B.C.) one of Rome's most
formidable opponents.
Croesum: king of Lydia from c. 560–546 B.C. According to
tradition, he was advised by Solon to 'count no man happy
until he is dead'. See Herodotus, 1.29.
spatia ultima: closing laps.

276-282 In 88 B.C., on Sulla's return, Marius had to flee from Rome. He
hid in a swamp at Minturnae in S Latium, but was caught and
imprisoned. After being released he made his way to Africa and
lived in a beggar's hut on the ruins of Carthage. (It would have
spoiled J's point to add that he later returned to Rome and held
a seventh consulship.)
hinc: from long life.
circumducto: the procession made a long circuit through the city.
opimam: 'glorious', a word often used of spoils.
Teutonico: referring to Marius' triumph over the Teutones and
Cimbri in 101 B.C.
vellet: was on the point of.

283-288 At Naples in 50 B.C. Pompey had a dangerous fever; it was much
to be desired, because it would normally have brought death, but
the misguided prayers of the Campanian towns prevailed, and he
survived — only to be decapitated two years later when coming
ashore at Pelusium in Egypt. Rome lost her freedom with
Pompey's death, hence her Fortuna was bound up with his.
victo: dat. (GL 345).
caput: J employs two meanings — 'life' with *servatum*, 'head'
with *abstulit*. Lentulus and Cethegus were executed for treason in
63 B.C.; their leader Catiline died in battle the following year.

291   *usque ad delicias votorum*: going to fanciful lengths in her
prayers.

292   *corripias*: deliberative subjunctive (W 109 n.2) 'why should you
find fault?'
Latona: mother of Diana and Apollo.

293   *Lucretia*: the wife of Collatinus, who killed herself after being
raped by Sextus Tarquinius. See Livy 1.57ff.

294-295 *Rutilae*: unknown.
Verginia: a beautiful girl who was killed by her father and so
saved from the lustful attentions of Appius Claudius. See Livy
3.44–51. We have printed Housman's emendation of the reading

atque suum, which may have arisen from the intermediate
corruption *otque suum.*

298-299 *licet*: although, with subjunctives *tradiderit . . . tribuat.*
horrida: 'rough' in the sense of 'simple' and 'austere'; it is linked
with *imitata* by *ac.*

300-301 *voltumque . . . ferventem*: i.e. blushing.
benigna: abl with *manu.*

303   *custode*: abl. of comparison with *potentior*; it refers to the
paedagogus. Strictly speaking, the subject of *conferre potest*,
like that of *tribuat* in v. 301, is external Nature; whereas the
factor which is *custode potentior* is internal nature or character.

304-305 Lit. 'the free-spending effrontery of the seducer'.

306-309 For the topos of tyrants and castration see Mayor's note.
Although J exaggerates, the practice clearly went on (at least in
the case of boys who were not free-born); for it was forbidden by
Domitian (Suetonius, *Dom.* 7), Nerva (Dio Cassius 68.2.4), and
Hadrian (Ulpian *Dig.* 48.8.4.2). Nero's bisexual activities are
mentioned in Suetonius, *Nero* 28.

308   *loripedem*: with weak misshapen legs.

309   *utero*: belly.

310   *iuvenis*: i.e. *fīliī.*
laetare: 2nd sing. imperative.

313   *irae debebit*: this is E.C.'s emendation of the unintelligible
reading *irati debet.* See *Bull. Inst. Class. Stud.* 13 (1966) 41.

313-314 'Nor will he (strictly "his luck") be more fortunate than the luck
of Mars so as never to be caught.' Mars was caught with Venus in
a trap laid by Vulcan. See *Odyssey* 8.266ff.

315   *ille dolor*: the husband's resentment. The *Lex Iulia de adulteriis*,
which applied in J's day, did not allow the aggrieved husband to
kill the adulterer if the latter was a freeborn Roman citizen. The
implication is that the other punishments mentioned were also
illegal.

317   *mugilis*: the grey mullet. This small wedge-shaped fish with stiff
spines was pushed into the culprit's anus so as to inflict the
maximum pain and humiliation. See Ellis on Catullus 15.19.

318   *Endymion*: a beautiful young shepherd or huntsman beloved of
        the moon, who watched over him as he slept in a cave on Mt.
        Latmus in Caria.
        dilectae etc.: 'he will fall for a married lady and become her
        lover.'

320   *fiet*: sc. *adulter*.

321   *negaverit*: potential subjunctive; for the tense see GL 257, W 119.

322   *haec*: this looks forward to *deterior femina*. Others take *sive . . .
        Catulla* with the previous question.

323   *illic*: i.e. *in inguinibus*. That organ rules her personality.

325-328 *grave propositum*: 'strict way of life;' cf. 5.1, 9.21.
        Hippolytus: a young man averse to sex. His step-mother Phaedra
        (the Cretan woman of v. 327) tried to seduce him. When she
        failed she told her husband Theseus that Hippolytus had tried to
        rape her. Theseus pronounced a curse which resulted in his son's
        death. *Bellerophon* was similarly accused by Sthenoboea, the wife
        of his host Proetus. As a punishment he was set to perform a
        series of perilous tasks. A line ending with a reference to Phaedra
        seems to have fallen out after v. 325; as it is, we can hardly tell
        that *haec* in v. 326 refers to her. Phaedra 'blushed with shame at
        the rebuff (*repulsā*) as if she had been scorned' — though in fact
        the rejection was due to Hippolytus' purity.
        se concussere: whipped themselves into a rage.

329   *pudor*: i.e. an injured *amour propre*, rather than an honourable
        sense of shame.

330   Supply *ei* before *cui*.
        Caesaris uxor: Messalina, wife of Claudius, conceived a passion
        for the consul designate, C. Silius, a married man, and went
        through a wedding ceremony with him. As a consequence they
        were both destroyed. See Tacitus, *Ann.* 11.12 and 26 ff.

332   *rapitur . . . extinguendus*: carried away to destruction by
        Messalina's eyes.

333-336 *dudum sedet*: she has been sitting for a long time (GL 230).
        flammeolo: the usual word is *flammeum* (a flame-coloured bridal
        veil); the diminutive is probably due to metrical convenience,
        though it also enhances the sarcastic tone. The (*lectus*) *genialis*
        is covered with purple because the bride is an empress.
        in hortis: probably the grounds once belonged to Lucullus; the
        lectus is placed here rather than in the atrium, because this is a

public ceremony (Tacitus, *Ann.* 11.30).

ritu . . . antiquo: this refers to the handing over of the dowry, not to the amount — in this case 1,000,000 sesterces. The *signatores* witnessed the marriage contract; the *auspex* pronounced a blessing.

337   *tu*: Silius.

338   *quid placeat dic*: state your decision.

339-340 In these mixed conditions the protasis puts forward a supposition, the apodosis states a certainty.

341   *contingat*: subjunctive, as if some horrible purpose were being worked out (GL 572).

343   *obsequere*: imperative.
        tanti: gen. of value.

344   *levius*: easier.
        putaris: fut. perfect.

347   *expendere*: to estimate; hence the indirect questions.

351   *magnaque*: this sounds rather weak. Housman suggested *vanaque* or *pravaque*. The latter might have been corrupted to *parvaque* and then 'miscorrected' to *magnaque*.

353   *qui pueri*: sc. *futuri sint*.
        qui: what sort of.

354   *et*: i.e. 'not only submit to what is appointed but *also* present a petition.' So Mayor. Or take *et* with the following *-que*. So Duff. The first presents a difficulty of logic, the second a difficulty of emphasis.

355   *divina*: fit for the gods. Note the effect of the diminutives.

358   *extremum*: sc. *munus*.
        ponat: generic subjunctive (W 155).

361   *labores*: i.e. those of Hercules, who was venerated by the Stoics.

362   *pluma*: collective singular; 'down cushions'.
        Sardanapalli: Latin form of Assurbanipal, king of Assyria 668–629 B.C. Stories of his luxury and effeminacy, common in the classical world, are derived from the lost account of Ctesias (see especially Diodorus 2.23–27), but receive no confirmation from

Assyrian sources.

363   *possis*: indefinite or generalizing 2nd person (W 119).

365   You have no divinity, (as men would realize) if they had any sense. 'The lively fancy of the Roman often employs the Ideal where we should expect the Unreal' (GL 596.2 remark 1); hence the present subjunctive here, when we might have expected the imperfect.

SUGGESTED EXERCISE

Compare *Sat.* 10 with Johnson's *The Vanity of Human Wishes.*

1.   Although the two poems are almost equal in length, the corresponding sections sometimes vary. Why do you think this is so?

2.   Do Johnson's omissions and alterations imply a different attitude to the subject?

3.   If so, is this connected in any way with religion? (The ending is especially important here.)

FURTHER READING

J. Butt and M. Lascelles in *New Light on Dr. Johnson*, ed. F. W. Hilles, Yale 1959.

D. Eichholz, 'The Art of Juvenal and his Tenth Satire', *Greece and Rome* n.s. 3 (1956) 61-69.

H. Gifford, 'The Vanity of Human Wishes', *Review of English Studies* 6 (1955) 157-165.

H. A. Mason (see bibliography).

N. Rudd, *Johnson's Juvenal*, Bristol Classical Press 1981.